A LETTER TO BALLYTURAN

MICHAEL GRANT

Best Wishes

Mac Grant

ACKNOWLEDGMENTS

Special thanks to my sharp-eyed copy editors, Sandi Nadolny and Elizabeth Grant for their efforts to ensure that I wrote what I meant to write. Of course, if there are any errors in the manuscript the fault is mine alone.

For of all sad words of tongue or pen,
the saddest are these: "It might have been!"

~ John Greenleaf Whittier ~

CHAPTER ONE

Fort Dix
November 3, 1945

An antsy Sergeant Matthew McCartan stood at the back of a long line of soldiers waiting to board the bus to New York City. He glanced at his watch for the third time in as many minutes. Why the hell isn't this damn line moving? He consoled himself with the thought that at least this would be the last time he would ever have to stand in line as a soldier again. For the past three years, he'd spend most of his time standing in line for everything from vaccinations for God-knows-what horrible diseases to K-rations and ammunition in places as far apart as Camp Claiborne in Louisiana and Sainte Mère Église in Normandy. Once again, he patted the thick manila folder in his jacket containing his separation papers, scarcely able to believe that he had finally been mustered out of the army after three years of fighting the war in Europe.

At five-foot ten, Matt McCartan was about average in height, but extremely thin—the result of almost two months in a field hospital in England recovering from shrapnel wounds. As a child, he had had bright red hair, but over the years it had darkened and now his close-cropped hair was more the color of rust. He was only twenty-two, but what he'd seen in the war had aged him. He looked at least ten years older and there was a wariness, a caution in the eyes that would stay with him for the rest of his life.

Finally, the line started to move. He found a seat toward the back of the bus next to a bleary-eyed master sergeant with a chest full of medals who surreptitiously snorted whisky from a silver flask. The sergeant offered it to him. "Want a pop?"

"No," Matt said a little too quickly.

The sergeant looked at him sideways. "For chrissake, kid," he said with a pronounced Brooklyn accent, "what are you so friggin' jumpy about? You're still in one piece and you're goin' home, ain't ya?"

Matt grunted in agreement and closed his eyes to avoid further conversation. He was going home all right, but there was no way for the sergeant to know that he was going home to his father's funeral. He had memorized the contents of the telegram he'd received three days earlier.

Sergeant Matthew McCartan
101st Airborne Division U.S. Army
Sorry to inform your father dead -(STOP)- Funeral
November 3 -(STOP)- All arrangements made -(STOP)-
Hope you will be there -(STOP)- Gus

The army, true to form, had tried to shaft him one last time. In the mustering out center, he was supposed to get an expedited emergency discharge because of a death in the family, but there was the typical SNAFU and the paperwork got lost. He'd made up his mind to go AWOL, but at the last minute, they found the papers. And so, here he was aboard a bus on his way into Manhattan and a funeral. He glanced at his watch again. If the bus didn't break down, he had just enough time to get there.

~~

Shouldering his duffle bag and taking the stairs two at a time, Matt came up out of the subway at Lexington Avenue and East 86th Street. It had been three years since he'd last been here. "Sauerkraut Boulevard," as it was affectionately called by the neighborhood people, still looked the same. Yet, in some ways it was different. As a kid growing up in Yorkville, 86th Street had been a magical playground for him and his friends.

As he hurried east toward First Avenue, he passed familiar landmarks that sent a flood of memories from his earlier life coursing through his mind. He passed the Lowe's Orpheum and the familiar smell of popcorn—either real or imagined—filled his nostrils, reminding him of how he and his friends spent every Saturday afternoon boisterously watching westerns and cartoons. A few doors down was the Horn & Hardart's, where they would go when they managed to pool enough pennies and nickels to get a cup of coffee and a roll. No one much liked coffee, but they all liked to crank the handle and watch it pour from the mouths of silver dolphins. Then there was that record shop that let you go into a booth and listen to a record before your bought it. Around the third record, the manager would realize they had no intention of buying anything and they'd be thrown out.

Good times. So long ago.

~~

As he jogged across Third Avenue, dodging a herd of yellow taxis, a noisy El train rattled overhead. He noticed that the Papaya stand was still there and wondered if they still had the best Papaya and hotdogs in the city. He was surprised to see that the Berlin bar was still open. After such a bloody war with Nazi Germany, he thought they might at least have changed the name.

He turned the corner into East 87th Street just in time to see six men carrying a casket up the stairs and into St. Joseph's Church. For the first time since he'd come off the bus at the Port Authority Terminal, he stopped dead in his tracks. With a start, he realized it was his father who was inside that casket.

At the top of the stairs stood a squat, heavyset man anxiously looking around. With his swarthy complexion and black, busy eyebrows, he looked almost menacing. But under those eyebrows were the wide, sensitive eyes of a child. Gus Conforti spotted Matt and rushed toward him.

"Mattie, thank God, you made it here in time." With tears glistening in his eyes, he hugged the young man. "Mattie, I'm so sorry. Your father... he went too soon... too soon..."

"Yeah, I know, Gus. What happened?"

Gus ran his hands through his thick hair. "I don't know. One minute he's operating the forklift, the next thing, it crashes into a pallet stacked with cases of beer. By the time I got to him, he was slumped over, dead. Just like that. The doctors said he took a heart attack."

Fifty-two, Matt thought. The old man was just fifty-two. It seemed kind of young but, then again, he'd seen men a lot younger die. Maybe these days, fifty-two qualified as old age. Before he could ask another question, a solemn-faced usher came out and called to Gus, "Mr. Conforti, the funeral's about to start."

~~

It had been over three years since Matt had set foot inside St. Joseph's Church, but nothing had changed. There was still the familiar sweet, cloying scent of incense, and the same oppressive quietness, punctured only by the hissing, whispered prayers of old women scattered about the cavernous church. Matt and Gus walked down the central aisle. He noticed there were only a handful of people seated in the front pews. Not surprising. The old man had no family, at least that he knew of. For that matter, he had no friends either, except for Gus Conforti. Parishioners, sprinkled throughout other parts of the church, elbowed each other and pointed at the young man in uniform as he came down the aisle, but Matt didn't notice. His eye were fixed on the coffin. He placed his hand gently on the highly polished casket and slid into the front pew.

With detached curiosity, he watched the funeral ritual unfold as the altar boys, carrying the tools of their trade—crucifix, candles and incense—took their positions around the casket, as he, himself, had done

countless times. What did they call the funeral ritual? *Smells and bells.*
The priest began to intone in Latin the familiar prayers for the dead. He
didn't recognize the elderly, pinched-faced man. As the priest droned on,
alternating in Latin and English, Matt thought he detected a German
accent. For some reason, that made him uneasy. He studied the faces of
the altar boys. He had been one of them from the fifth grade until
graduation, but they looked so young, so impossibly young. Had he ever
been that young?

His gaze drifted to the statue of the crucified Christ twisting on the
cross above the altar. He knew he should say a prayer, but he couldn't
remember one. Only the Latin words *mea culpa, mea culpa, mea maxima
culpa* flashed into his mind. When he'd gone into the army, he'd had
religion. In high school, he'd even entertained the thought of becoming a
priest. Now, that seemed so long ago. Somewhere along the way he'd lost
his religion and his faith in God. Where did he lose it? Normandy?
Bastogne? Sainte Marie-du-Mon? Or maybe it was when they liberated
the concentration camp at Landsberg. He looked away from the crucifix.
What did it matter? It was gone. All gone.

~~

At the sprawling Calvary Cemetery in Queens, Matt stood at the open
gravesite and listened to the priest offer kind and complimentary words
about a man he had probably never met. Matt's eyes drifted to the
headstone and he read the words already engraved there:

Grace McCartan
1900-1923
Died that another might live
She rests with the angels

He was "that another". Once again, he wondered if that was why his
father, a man of few words to begin with, had so little to say to him. All
his life, he'd sensed a hostility in the old man toward him. Was that just
the way he was, or did he blame his son for the death of his wife? Matt
had always wondered, but he never had the courage to ask that question.
And now it was too late.

He knew he would have to order a headstone inscription for his father,
but what would it say? Barry McCartan born 1893, died 1945. That part
was easy. But what else could it say? Here lies my father, a man of few
words? Her lies my loving father…?

He was pulled away from his musing by the movement of cemetery
workmen lowering the casket into the ground. At a nod from the priest,
Matt stepped forward and dropped a single rose into the hole.

4

And it was done.

As they moved away from the gravesite, Gus introduced Matt to the handful of men who had been in church and who had come to the cemetery. They were all men who had worked with his father at the Ruppert Brewery. Matt was astonished by how highly they spoke of his father. A great man… Give you the shirt off his back… Wonderful sense of humor… Were they talking about his father? Barry McCartan? Could they be talking about the same taciturn man that he had grown up with? He was prepared to chalk up their praise to politeness and the need to say the proper thing to the son of a coworker, but there was no feigning the tears in the eyes or the breaking in the voices. No, these men, for reasons an astonished Matt could only imagine, seemed to genuinely like his father.

~~

Back in Yorkville, Matt and Gus headed directly for the Black Forest, Barry McCartan's old hangout on First Avenue. The owner, Otto Schmidt, had long since died, but his wife, Klara, a crusty no-nonsense woman of sixty, ran the place with iron Teutonic efficiency and order.

She was behind the bar and spotted them coming through the door. "Ya, will you look at you, Matthew McCartan," she said, coming from behind the bar and wiping her hands on her apron. "All grown up and looking so excellent in your uniform. But Gott in Himmel, so skinny." She gave him a hug and brushed an imaginary speck from his shoulder. "Matthew, I am so sorry about your father."

"Thanks, Klara."

Gus glared at the array of taps behind the bar. "I see you still don't have Ruppert on tap."

She waved a hand in dismissal. "Ach, don't start that again, for goodness sake." She poked Matt in the chest. "Just because he works for Ruppert, he thinks it's the best beer in the world."

"Well, it is," Gus responded indignantly.

"Look, will you? I have got Blatz, Schlitz, Pabst, Rheingold, and Ballantine. It's enough already."

"And not one of them compares to Ruppert."

She pointed to her temple and made a circular motion with her index finger. "These Ruppert men, they are all cuckoo in the head."

Mumbling a protest, Gus ordered a pitcher of Schlitz and took it into the back room and sat down opposite Matt.

"It's not much of a homecoming, is it?" he said, pouring the beer.

"It's not the way I planned it."

Even as he said it, he realized that was wrong. The truth was, he hadn't planned anything. Like the other GIs in his outfit, he had been

5

counting the days until his discharge, especially during the last year of the war. It was exciting, but at the same time frightening. Everyone could sense the war was winding down and no one wanted to be the last soldier to die on the last day of the war. Some of his buddies even talked wistfully about receiving that "million dollar" wound that wouldn't kill or maim them, but would get them sent back stateside. But as far as his plans for the future? He didn't have any. And he knew why. He'd listened to too many young men talk about the future only to die in the next firefight. He'd decided it was bad luck to plan for the future. It was tempting fate.

"What are you going to do now, Mattie? Thinking about getting a job?"

Matt took a sip of beer and frowned. The beer, even in wartime Germany, was far superior to this. "No, I haven't given it much thought."

"Then don't worry," Gus said, patting Matt's hand. "I talked to the big shots at the brewery. They said they'll always have a job for Barry McCartan's kid."

There it was again. Even the "big shots" at Ruppert must have liked my father. How strange.

"Gus, tell me about my dad," Matt said, suddenly.

Gus was taken aback by the abruptness of the request. "Matt, what could I tell you about your own father that you don't already know?"

"The truth is, I don't know much about him. We never talked much. Just the necessities—'Did you eat?' 'What time will you be home?' 'Don't forget to pick up milk.' That was about it."

Gus stared at him with the kind of bewildered expression that Matt had seen before. Every time he mentioned to someone that his father barely spoke to him, they thought he was exaggerating. But he wasn't. They really didn't talk. Ever. Over the years, he'd gotten used to the silence at dinnertime and the long, quiet evenings listening to the radio. In time, he had come to actually enjoy the silence. It allowed him to to live undisturbed in his own mind.

Gus stared into his glass. "Your dad," he began slowly, "was different. It's true, he didn't have a lot to say, but he was actually a very funny guy. A real dry sense of humor, ya know? And a hard worker. I'll give him that. Your old man never shied away from doing any kind of work at the brewery. Not one time. Everybody respected him for that..." Gus's voice trailed off and he shrugged. "I don't know what else to say, Mattie."

"Did he ever talk about relatives?"

"Nah. Why?"

"Because I don't know if I have relatives. For all I know, there might be a whole clan of McCartan's living in the Bronx. I just don't know."

"Geez, I can't help you there, Mattie."

After a long, awkward silence, Gus looked at his watch. "Hey, look, I gotta be getting home. Angie will kill me if I'm late for supper. Mattie, why don't you come home with me and have a real home cooked meal for a change. I think she's making lasagna. It's gotta be better than that stuff they fed you in the army. Come on, whadda ya say?"

"I'll pass, Gus. But thanks for the offer. Maybe some other time."

"Yeah, right. I understand. You got things to think about." Uncomfortable expressing emotion, Gus shook Matt's hand and averted his eyes to the half-empty pitcher of beer on the table. "That's real crappy beer, you know?" He cleared his throat. "Well, anyways… again, Mattie, I'm so sorry about your father and, you know, all that."

"Yeah, I know. Thanks for making the funeral arrangements, Gus. I wasn't sure I was gonna get back in time."

"Hey—" Gus almost said *anytime*, but he caught himself. "I was happy to help," he muttered.

~~

Matt stayed in the back room and finished off the pitcher. He knew he should go to the apartment and begin to sort through the old man's stuff, but he just wasn't ready for that. Klara saved him from having to make a decision. She came into the back room carrying two small glasses and sat down across from him. "Here, Matthew," she said, sliding a glass toward him. "A little schnapps. It's very good for the heart, ya?"

Matt took a sip of the strong liquor and it burned all the way down his throat. It felt good. After a moment, he said, "Klara, what do you know about my father?"

She gave him the same puzzled look that Gus had given him. "Well, I don't know what to say, Matthew. I can tell you he was never a problem in the bar. He could hold his liquor, your father. Not that he ever drank too much, mind you. He kept to himself, but he was friendly enough."

"He came from Ireland. Did he ever talk about that?"

"Nein, I can't say that he did."

"How about relatives?"

Klara shook her head.

Matt was getting more desperate. "My mother. Did he ever mention her?"

The old woman looked away, embarrassed for both of them. "Nein. Look, Matthew, the way men behave in bars is sometimes very different from the way they behave at home. I suppose that's why they go to bars, so they can be… I don't know"—she shrugged, searching for the proper word—"themselves."

"I guess so," he said, not satisfied with that explanation. "It's just that since I've been away, I've had a lot of time to think about him and I still can't figure him out. He was Irish, but he never said a word about Ireland to me or anyone else that I know. Every year, the Saint Patrick's Day parade ends on 86th Street, just a few blocks from here, but to my knowledge he never once attended the parade. Why did he move into Yorkville, a predominately German neighborhood? And why did he decide to hang out here, a German bar, instead of one the dozens of Irish bars in the neighborhood? And his best friend—his only friend—is Italian. Klara, I don't understand any of it. I'd made up my mind that as soon as I got back, I would confront him and ask him these questions, but now..."

Klara nodded and silently sipped her schnapps.

Matt realized he was was making her uncomfortable. Changing the subject, he said, "So, Klara, how have you been?"

She wiped her hands on her apron and her eyes misted up. "It's been a very difficult four years, Matthew. During the war, there was a lot of anti-German feelings around here. More than once, I had hooligans come in here and break up the bar, calling us Nazis and Gestapo and worse. I know Yorkville has a reputation for being a haven for Nazi supporters, but not every German agreed with Hitler. If Otto and I had had a son, I would have been proud to have him join the army the way you did and fight that swine, Hitler."

She stood up and patted her severe bun. "Das ist Genug. Enough of such talk. She looked him up and down. "Matthew, you are too skinny. I will make you a nice sandwich. I have some wonderful liverwurst from Schaller and Weber and some fresh pumpernickel from..."

Matt stood up. "No, thanks, Klara. I've got to be going." It was time to go to the apartment. He'd put it off long enough.

She gave him a hug. "Well, you take care of yourself and don't be a stranger, you hear me?"

"I won't," he said, suddenly realizing he would probably continue the old man's ritual and hangout at the Black Forest. And for some reason, he found that thought troubling.

CHAPTER TWO

The nondescript, five-story brick tenement, constructed in the last quarter of the 19th century, was barely indistinguishable from the other buildings that lined both sides of Second Avenue. He pushed through the vestibule door and into the hallway where he was assailed by the pleasantly familiar smells of cabbage and knockwurst.

Slowly, he made his way up the four floors and with each floor a flood of memories came rushing back. In his minds eye, he saw him and his best friend, Neil, racing up and down the stairs in a frantic game of tag and getting thrown out of the building by the irate super. He remembered the loud fights that came from apartment 3S and wondered if the couple still lived there or if they had killed each other in the meantime.

He stopped outside apartment 4N and gave himself a moment to collect his thoughts. It had been three years since he'd set foot inside and for some reason he was suddenly apprehensive. What did he expect to find? The apartment had been the only home he had ever known and, in spite of his father's coldness, he'd spent a mostly pleasant childhood here.

He put the key in the lock and stepped inside. The railroad apartment—so called because all five rooms were connected in a straight line—was dark. He moved to the center of the kitchen and, as he had done countless times, unerringly reached up and pulled the overhead light cord. He blinked at the sudden brightness and looked around. Nothing had changed. It was as if he'd just gone out to pick up a quart of milk. There was a bowl of apples and bananas on the table-clothed table. There was not a dish or cup in the sink. The curtains hung straight and pressed. And then he remembered: His father had always been exceedingly neat. For as long as he could recall, the apartment was always spotless, nothing ever out of place. He'd been in plenty of friends' apartments where there had been a mother present, but he'd never seen any apartment neater than his own.

He put his duffle bag down and walked into the next room off the kitchen—his father's bedroom—and smiled. As he had always done, the old man had made the bed before he'd gone to work the morning he'd died. Matt opened the closet and immediately detected the faint scent of Old

Spice. His eyes swept the clothes neatly hung. That old blue suit was still there. He glanced up and there on the top shelf was his father's old suitcase where he kept his important papers. He quickly closed the closet, not wanting for the moment to think about what was in that suitcase.

The next room was his. His Yankee pennant was still on the wall over his bed. He continued toward the front of the apartment, passing one more bedroom that they'd never used, and finally, he came into the small, but comfortable, living room. He switched on a lamp and sat down on the couch, suddenly exhausted. He looked at his watch. It was almost midnight. He'd been up for over twenty hours.

He thought again about the old suitcase. Should he open it now? He decided it could wait till morning. He stretched out on the couch and promptly fell into a deep sleep.

~~

Just before dawn, he awoke with a start, confused and disoriented. It took him a moment to realize he was in his own apartment. He sat up and rubbed his eyes. The city was coming alive and he could hear the familiar rumble of buses, trucks, and cars moving up and down Second Avenue. It suddenly occurred to him that he was hungry and he realized he hadn't eaten anything since yesterday morning. Powered eggs and very bad coffee hardly counted as breakfast.

He went into the kitchen and opened the refrigerator. There were the usual staples—milk, butter, eggs, a six-pack of Knickerbocker, wrapped cold cuts, and assorted dinner leftovers. He sniffed the open bottle of milk and was pleased that it hadn't spoiled. Ten minutes later he sat down at the kitchen table with a bowl of Corn Flakes and a cup of coffee.

By his third cup, he realized he was stalling. But why? Was he afraid to open the suitcase because he might find out something about his father that he didn't know? Or perhaps worse, that nothing in that suitcase would help him understand who his father was.

He carried the dusty, battered suitcase into the kitchen and placed it on the table. He was surprised to see a small lock on it. He didn't remember seeing that before and wondered why his father, who lived alone, would feel the need to lock up the old suitcase.

He found a screwdriver in the junk drawer. As he was about to snap the lock, he hesitated, suddenly feeling like a voyeur. After all, in his entire life, his father never offered to share the contents of the suitcase with him. Why? Another question with no answer. Dismissing his misgivings, he snapped the lock off and opened the lid.

There was surprisingly little inside, mostly stacks of old gas and electric bills, and faded articles cut out from newspapers. He scanned the stories, but they didn't seem to relate to anything important. There were several faded photographs, mostly of his mother in her younger years. Among them was a photo of another girl who looked to be in her teens. Judging by the old-fashioned dress she wore, this photo was much older than the others. She was facing the sun and had one hand over her eyes, shielding her face from the sun, making it difficult to see what she looked like. Still, Matt was fairly certain it wasn't his mother. The young girl was standing on a hill. Behind her was a vast expanse of water. He turned the photo over. In faded handwriting he could barely make out 1915 and only the letters MA.

He put that photo aside and opened an envelope stuffed with more photos. He stared at the contents in astonishment. There were dozens and dozens photographs of him from the time he was in a baby carriage all the way up to the time he graduated from high school. Matt didn't even know his father had taken pictures of him at his graduation and he had no idea the old man kept all these photographs of him growing up.

He held the suitcase upside down and shook it. But there was nothing else inside. He sat back, disappointed. He didn't know what he'd expected to find, but, except for the photos of him, nothing in the suitcase gave a clue as to who his father really was. As he was about to place the contents back into the suitcase, he ran his hands around the side pockets and felt something. He pulled out a yellowed envelope. It was addressed to his father at a Brooklyn address he didn't recognize. The ink-faded return address was—Matt's heart pounded in his chest—*Ireland*. He couldn't make out the name of the person, but it came from a place called *Ballyturan*.

~~

Later that afternoon, Matt stopped at his old hangout, the Emerald Isle, on Second Avenue. As soon as he came into the bar, a middle-aged, ruddy-faced bartender let out a shout, startling the few patrons who were quietly sipping their beers and reading newspapers.

"Jaysus, if it isn't himself, Mattie McCartan, back from the war."

The bartender's wet hand grabbed Matt's in a vice-like grip. "Mattie, it's damn good to see your back safe and sound. Thanks be to Jaysus."

"Thanks, Sean. It's good to be back." He looked around. Usually by this time, most of his friends would be here. "Where is everybody? Timmy, Frankie, Gene? I haven't seen these guys since I went away. Do they still come in here?"

Sean frowned and busied himself rubbing his hands with a bar rag. "Ah, things have changed since you've been away, Mattie. You know, the war and all."

Matt saw the troubled expression on the bartender's face and felt a lump forming in his stomach. "Timmy and Frankie and Gene—are they..."

"Mattie, why don't you go into the back room. We set up sort of a memorial-like thing for all you boys who went overseas."

As memorials went, it wasn't much. Just a small blackboard, the kind the bar used to write out the daily lunch specials, flanked by two American flags. The blackboard was filled with names. As Matt approached, the blur of chalk marks began to coalesce into real names. Cpl. Gregory Mullins USMC killed in action August 1942... Seaman William Burke USN killed in action September 1943... Matt knew them. He went to school with them, but they weren't his personal friends. His eyes scanned the list, looking for his friends—and he found one: Sgt. Timothy O'Leary USA killed in action January 1944. He studied the name with detachment. After seeing so many of his buddies killed during the war, he had become numbed to death. He could still feel regret, but not grief.

He was relieved that Frankie and Gene's names weren't there. For certain he knew his best friend, Neil Walsh, wouldn't be on the list. Of all his friends, only Neil had been kept out of the service by perforated eardrums, the side effects of a childhood bout of Scarlet Fever. The last he heard, Neil had been working for Con Ed.

He went back to the bar and ordered a beer. "Does Neil still come in, Sean?"

"Aye, that he does." The bartender looked at the wall clock. "He should be coming through that door any minute now."

"Sean, have you ever heard of a town in Ireland called Ballyturan?"

"What part of Ireland is it?"

"I don't know."

"Jaysus, Mattie, Ireland may be small, but there's a fearful lot of cities, towns, and villages crammed into it. Sure it could be ten miles from me own town and I wouldn't know it, unless they had a football team. Then, I'd know it for sure."

Just then, the door opened and a tall, pudgy man in a dark blue suit came in. It took Matt a moment to recognize his friend, but Neil recognized Matt right away.

He rushed to Matt and grabbed him in a bear hug. "Mattie, Mattie, goddamn, it's good to see you." He pulled back to get a look at his friend. "Damn, it looks like I gained the weight you lost. Sean," he called out to the bartender, "give us a pitcher. Me and Matt have a lot of catching up to do."

In the back room, Neil poured the beer. "You got out of the army pretty quick, didn't you? I've been reading that they're really backed up with the demobilization."

"That's true. But they got some kind of crazy point system. I got wounded and apparently that counts for a lot. Also, my dad just died and…"

"Oh, geez, I'm so sorry, Matt. I didn't hear anything. No one told me."

"It was quick and low key. No wake. Gus took care of the arrangements. He was buried yesterday."

"Hey, if there's anything I can do…"

"No, I'm good."

After an awkward pause, Neil said, "So, Mattie, did you see a lot of action?"

"Yeah, I guess so. We used to joke that the Screaming Eagles was the only outfit the war planners could remember when they were drawing up battle plans. We seemed to be in the middle of everything."

"I wish I'd gone, Mattie. You don't know how guilty I feel about not having done my part."

"Don't sweat it, Neil. Hey, if you can't hear the tanks coming, you're dead meat."

"Yeah, still…"

Matt's eyes flicked to the blackboard behind Neil. "I see Timmy caught it."

"Yeah. Anzio. I stay in touch with his mom. She took it pretty hard."

"So, are you still with Con Ed?" Mattie asked, trying to change the subject to something not so morbid.

"Yeah, I'm a supervisor now. Good steady job. Good future. How about you? You got anything lined up?"

"I think I can get a job at Rupperts."

Neil frowned. "Rupperts. Forget about that. I can get you a job at Con Ed. Better money and damn good security."

Matt grinned. "Yeah, but no free beer in the employee taproom."

"You got me there." Neil refilled their glasses. "So, what are your plans now that you're home?"

Matt found himself getting irritated by that question. Why did everyone want to know what his plans were? He shrugged. "Nothing in the immediate future. I got a lot of back pay I couldn't spend in Europe, so I can afford to goof off for a while. I intend to sleep late, stay up late, and eat all those things I couldn't get in the past three years."

"Sounds like a plan to me."

"Oh, and I might also go to college."

Neil chuckled. "You? A college man?"

"Maybe. At Dix, I heard some guys talking about something called the GI Bill. Apparently, the government will pay vets to go to college."

"That sounds like a damn good deal to me."

"Yeah, I'm gonna look into it. Of course, if the army has anything to with it it'll be one big SNAFU."

"Well, at least look into it." Neil looked at his watch. "Hey, I gotta run, Matt. I got a date."

"Oh, yeah, anything serious?"

Neil reddened. "Maybe. She's a terrific gal."

"Well, good for you. When do I get to meet her?"

"Soon. Hey, I'll meet you back here tomorrow. We're not finished catching up on the past. You got any plans for the rest of the day?"

"I'm going to the library."

"What the hell for?"

"It's a long story."

~~

Matt went into the library and headed for the reference desk. A middle-aged woman with thick glasses looked up. "Yes, may I help you?"

"I hope so. I'm trying to find a town in Ireland called Ballyturan."

"Well, that shouldn't be too difficult to find."

She directed him to a table in the reading room and went off to collect reference books. Five minutes later, she was back with an armful of big, bulky atlases. "You can start with these. If you don't find what your looking for, come back and see me."

The biggest and bulkiest book, the World Atlas, had a map of Ireland, but it showed only the larger cities and towns. He had better luck with the third book, a smaller atlas of Europe. He ran his finger down the indexed list of cities and towns and—there it was: Ballyturan A14. He flipped to the map of Ireland and found Ballyturan, a small dot on the Dingle Peninsula. He read the entry.

Ballyturan (population: 165) is located on the Dingle Peninsula, which stretches 30 miles into the Atlantic Ocean from Ireland's southwest coast. Ballyturan is a small fishing and farming village bound on the north by mountains and on the south by sea cliffs and sandy beaches.

For a long time, Matt studied the map, wondering if his father came from this village or if he just knew someone who did. He tried to imagine his father living there and wondered why he would have left.

~~

For the next several days, Matt couldn't get the image of the map out of his mind. And the more he thought about it, the more intrigued he became and the more questions began to crowd his mind. Did his father have family there? What did he do there? Why did he leave? Why did he never talk about it? But then, angrily, he would shake those thoughts loose from his mind. What was he thinking? He didn't even know if his father came from Ballyturan. And why was he wasting his time thinking about it in the first place?

The answer came to him one morning after a restless night of unsettling dreams about his father, the war, and the village of Ballyturan—which kept morphing into the bombed-out villages in the French countryside he'd marched through. Over a cup of coffee, he started to sort it out in his mind. When he'd gone off to war, he was only nineteen, too intimidated to confront his father and ask all the questions that had been bottled up inside him for as long as he could remember. He'd grown up a lot in those past three years. He'd seen enough death and destruction to last a lifetime. He'd also listened enviously to endless stories from his buddies about their mothers, fathers, brothers, and sisters, and he felt shame. How could he tell them that his father never spoke to him? It was true that some guys described their fathers as drunken bastards who beat them, but there were just as many who spoke highly of their parents. Listening to those conversations, Matt had made up his mind that, one way or another, when he got home, he would insist on his father answering every one of his questions. But, of course, that wouldn't happen now.

At the kitchen table, as he was finishing his fourth cup of coffee, he made up his mind. He had to at least try to find out who his father really was. But how? Where would he start? He retrieved the old suitcase from the closet and dumped the contents on the kitchen table. Thinking he might have missed something the first time, he read every newspaper article with great care and examined every piece of paper and every photograph. Maybe somewhere in that pile was a clue as to who his father was. But after carefully scrutinizing everything, the only clue—if he could call it that—was the faded envelope with the return address of Ballyturan.

He got a Knickerbocker from the refrigerator and sat back down at the table. As he sipped the beer, he stared at the contents from the suitcase, trying to think of his next step, but he kept drawing a blank. On his third beer, as he was fingering the faded envelope, it finally came to him. He would write a letter. But to whom? He had no name, no address, just the village of Ballyturan. He doubted a village of a hundred and sixty-five people would have a mayor or any other official, so who could he address the letter to?

"The priest," he suddenly said aloud, slamming the bottle on the table. That was it. He'd fought his way through dozens of villages in France,

Belgium, and Germany. And in every village, great or small, there was always a church. He would write to the village priest.

He rummaged through the kitchen drawers looking for a pen and writing paper, but he quickly realized he was wasting his time. His father never wrote letters. Why would he have writing paper? Matt rushed up to the Woolworth's on Third Avenue. As he was trying to decide which package of writing paper to buy, it occurred to him that, in addition to writing the parish priest, it would be a good idea to enclose additional letters and ask the priest to pass them on to anyone who might know something about his father. He bought two packages of writing paper and envelopes.

He rushed back home and sat down at the kitchen table, puzzling over what to write. He wasn't an experienced letter writer and he was slightly intimidated at the thought of writing to a priest. After several false starts, he finally wrote:

> *December 12, 1945*
> *To the Parish Priest of Ballyturan,*
> *My name is Matthew McCartan and I live in New York City. I have just recently buried my father, Barry McCartan. I believe he may have come from your village, or knew someone who did. I believe he came to the United States around 1916. I was hoping, that if you know anything about my father, you will write me at the above address.*
> *In addition, if it wouldn't be too much trouble, could you please distribute the enclosed letters enclosed to anyone in the village who might have known my father. Thank you for your help.*
> *Sincerely,*
> *Matt McCartan*

His second letter, which he copied a dozen more times, said:

> *December 12, 1945*
> *To Whom It May Concern:*
> *My name is Matthew McCartan and I live in New York City. I just recently buried my father, Barry McCartan. I believe he may have come from your village. I believe he came to the United States around 1916. I was hoping that if you know anything about my father, you will write me at the above address.*

Thanking you in advance, sincerely,
Matt McCartan

Afraid that he might decide this was all a wild goose chase and change his mind, he put everything in a large manila envelope, addressed it to Parish Priest of Ballyturan, County Kerry, Ireland, and rushed off to the post office.

CHAPTER THREE

Ballyturan
Ireland

The postman, an energetic young man in his mid-twenties, hurriedly pedaled his bicycle up the hill and skidded to a stop in front of a cottage adjacent to a diminutive church. Barely able to contain his excitement, he thumped on the red painted door with the flat of his palm.

A wide-eyed, thickset woman with gray hair tied up in a bun, opened the door. "For the love of God, Paddy, are you trying to break the door down all together?"

The young postman waved a large manila folder in front of her. "'Tis a letter from America. And will you look at the size of it."

"And who's it for?"

"It's addressed to the Parish Priest of Ballyturan, County Kerry, Ireland. And isn't this the address of our very own Father Aloysius Dunne?"

"Give it here." The old woman's eyes widened when she saw the name on the return address. "Jaysus, Mary, and Joseph..." she muttered, slamming the door in the surprised postman's face.

Sixty-eight-year-old Father Aloysius Dunne a short, rotund man with wispy gray hair, was in his cramped study reading the Irish Times when the old housekeeper barged in. He put the paper down and peered at her over his reading glasses. "What is it, Nora? You look like you've seen the devil himself."

"Not far from it." She placed the envelope in front of him. "It's from America and will you look who sent it."

Dunne leaned forward, read the return address, and fell back in his chair as though he'd been physically struck. "Who else has seen this?" he asked in a hoarse whisper.

"Just that daft postman, Paddy."

The priest studied the envelope, trying to decide if he even wanted to open it. Finally, he said, "Leave me, Nora. I'll tend to this."

After the old woman left, the priest took off his glasses and rubbed his eyes. He stood up and paced his tiny study, glancing at the envelope on his

18

desk from time to time as though it were a malignant presence. Finally, heaving a great sigh, he sat down, tore open the envelope and read the letter.

~~

Half way up the steep and winding gravel road leading to Squire Liam Kerrigan's imposing mansion, a wheezing Father Dunne had to stop to catch his breath. Leaning against a thick oak, he took the opportunity, as he always did, to admire the most beautiful structure in all of County Kerry. Built in the early part of the eighteenth century and surrounded by stately oaks and elms, the house epitomized classical Georgian construction—perfectly proportioned, restrained, and exuding purity and eloquence.

Having caught his breath, he continues up the road to the manor house. Still wheezing, he banged the large brass lion's head door knocker. A young woman dressed in the black and white livery of a parlor maid opened the door.

"I'm here to see the squire. He's expecting me."

The three men waiting for him in the spacious library were dwarfed by the fifteen-foot walls, which were lined with expensive leather-bound books, and an enormous fireplace at one end of the room. The older of the three men, a distinguished looking man in his late seventies, was Liam Kerrigan. The squire, as he liked to be called, was unquestionably the richest man on the Dingle Peninsula. He'd inherited most of his wealth from a long line of rapacious landlord ancestors, but as a shrewd businessman with barely a nodding acquaintance with ethics and honesty, he'd managed to dramatically increase his fortune over the years by investing in farming, banking, and real estate.

The second man was in his fifties, brawny and short of stature. Brian Heaney was the owner of Ballyturan's only butcher shop. Dressed in the worn, baggy wool clothing of a tradesman, he looked out of place in such elegant surroundings.

Looking equally out of place was the third man, John Twomey, a local farmer, whose muddy boots were soiling the fine Persian carpet underfoot.

An irritated Kerrigan sat down behind his ornate desk. "I'm a very busy man, Dunne. What is so important that you had to see us right away?"

Without a word the priest took Matt's letter out of his pocket and placed it on the desk.

Kerrigan read the letter and looked up sharply. "Why did he write this letter?"

"Who? Who wrote what letter?" Heaney said, snapping up the letter and reading it. "Oh, Jaysus Christ..." he said, slowly putting it back on the desk.

"Now, now, they'll be no taking the Lord's name in vain in my presence," the priest admonished Heaney.

"I'm sorry, Father. But, I must ask the same question. Why did this man write this letter?"

Twomey snapped up the letter and read it. Red-faced, he waved it at the priest, accusingly. "You said it was over when he left. Is yer man here trying to stir up trouble after all these years?"

"I don't know," the priest said, tugging at his stiff Roman collar. "Maybe there's nothing to it. Maybe he's like a lot of Yanks who get the sudden, foolish urge to trace their ancestors. The lot of them are convinced that they come from a long line of Irish kings," he said in disgust. "More likely it's just a long line of ignorant peasants and felons."

"Who else knows about this letter?" Kerrigan asked. "Has Hugh Cleary seen it?"

The priest shook his head vehemently. "Sure don't you know I'd never show such a letter to Hugh Cleary, and him being Barry McCartan's best friend. No one has seen the contents of this letter except us four and Paddy the postman."

"Well what are we gonna do about this?" an anxious Heaney asked, running his thick-fingered hand through his course hair.

"I'll tell you what we're going to do with it." Kerrigan snatched the letter from Twomey's hand. Rolling it in a ball, he went to the fireplace and hurled it in. As the fire consumed the letter, he turned to the priest. "Where are those other letters?"

"At the rectory."

"Go back there at once and burn them straight away."

"But what if he comes here?" a now near frantic Heaney asked.

Kerrigan shot him a withering glance. "Get hold of yourself, man. He says in the letter he's not even sure his father came from here. When he receives no response to his letters, he'll assume he's been barking up the wrong tree and that will put an end to it."

The disgruntled men left, not at all swayed by Kerrigan's assurance.

~~

Three days a week, Cathleen Mullen came to the rectory to help the arthritic Nora clean and cook. Earlier in the day, as she was was dusting the parlor, Father Dunne burst out of his study and hurried out of the rectory as though the devil, himself, was after him. After scrubbing the pots in the kitchen and doing the washing and ironing the linens, she suddenly remembered that the old priest didn't like her dusting the study when he was there. Now, she decided, would be a good time to do it.

After dusting the bookcases, she turned her attention to his messy desk. As she was moving a stack of letters, she happened to notice the signature at the bottom of one of a stack of letters and inhaled sharply. McCartan. She knew that name. Curious to see what he wanted, Cathleen quickly read the letter. She thumbed through the stack and saw that there were a dozen identical letters all addressed To Whom It May Concern. Deciding that her friend Claire should see it, she took the top letter, quickly folded it, and stuffed it in her apron pocket.

She continued cleaning the room and a few minutes later, a wheezing and harried Father Dunne barged into the room. He went directly to his desk and picked up the stack of letters. Cathleen froze. Had he counted them? Would he count them again? Just then, he looked up, startled, noticing Cathleen for the first time. "What are you doing here, girl?" he asked, gruffly.

"Just dusting, Father."

"You'll do that later. Now go help Nora in the kitchen."

Cathleen curtsied and hurriedly left the study, glad to be out of there.

Later that afternoon, after Father Dunne had left to visit a sick parishioner, Cathleen went back into the study to finish her dusting. The stack of letters was gone from the desk and there in the fireplace, which she'd just cleaned, were the charred remains of the letters. For reasons she couldn't imagine, Father Dunne had burned them.

CHAPTER FOUR

After a supper that he barely touched, a troubled Father Dunne retired to his study, utterly exhausted and distraught over the business of that letter from America. With a trembling hand he poured himself a generous dram of Bushmills. To ward off the chill that pained his arthritic bones, he pulled his chair up close to the warmth of the fire. Sitting down heavily in his comfortable old chair, his mind churned with the questions that had been troubling him since he'd seen that cursed letter. Why had the McCartan boy written the letter? What were his motives? Why would he want to stir up trouble that had been put to rest all those years ago? As he sipped the whisky and stared vacantly into the leaping yellow and red flames, his mind drifted back to that day so many years ago. Back in 1916...

~~

"Bless me Father, for I have sinned," whispered the soft, trembling voice of Maeve Cafferty.

"And how long has it been since your last confession, my child?"

Father Dunne always pretended not to know who was on the other side of the screen, but after a short while in a small village like Ballyturan, it was not difficult to recognize every voice from the youngest child to the oldest crone. He'd also become acutely attuned to the tone in their voices, which told him who was there merely to fulfill the requirements of the sacrament, and who was there to divulge deep and deadly sins.

"It's been two month since my last confession."

"Well, that is far too long," he said, crossly. He would have chastised her more, but from her tone he knew she was here for something more serious than missing confession for two months. He closed his eyes and pictured the dark-haired girl he saw at Mass every Sunday. Maeve Cafferty was a feisty one. Too feisty for her own good. Still, her previous confessions were always perfunctory recitations of the usual venal offenses—I lied three times... I stole a cabbage from a neighbor's field... I talked back to my mother... That was it. Nothing more serious than what any young girl of her age would have to confess. So what deadly mortal sin, he wondered, could a young girl, no more than twenty-four, have committed?

Still, sensing a foreboding premonition, he took a deep breath and said, "All right my child, confess your sins."

There was a long, long pause. He jerked his head to the right and peered through the darkened screen, half-expecting to see her gone. But in the gloom on the other side of the screen, he saw her shadowy image, motionless, and weeping softly.

"I've... I've committed a deadly mortal sin, Father. I..." At this point, she broke down and the rest of her words poured out in an unintelligible babble of sobs and sniffles.

"There, there, my child," he whispered. "There is no sin, no matter how terrible, that God in his infinite mercy will not forgive."

"I'm pregnant," she blurted out.

His head snapped back as though he'd been slapped in the face. Jaysus, Mary, and Saint Joseph. Not that. Please, dear God, not that.

"Who did this to you?" he hissed.

"I... I can't tell you, Father..."

"In the name of all the saints, do you mean to tell me that you have no idea who the father is? What kind of girl..."

"No, no... I know who the father is. I just can't tell you who he is."

"You'll tell me, Maeve Cafferty, or they'll be no absolution from me. And I warn you, my girl, if you step out of this confessional and are struck dead, you'll die with a terrible mortal sin on your soul and you'll burn in Hell for all eternity."

She started to weep again and her body was racked with convulsive sobs. All that caterwauling irritated him. It was always the same with this lot. They had no difficulty committing the sin, but they had all the difficulty in the world confessing it and repenting it. At least her weeping gave him a chance to regain his composure. But now, his mind was racing. He knew this would bring scandal to the village and a black mark against the church—and him. He would have to do something straight away. But what? But what?

He cleared his throat and in slow, measured tones said, "Maeve Cafferty, I'll give you one last chance to unburden your soul. If I'm to give you absolution for this terrible sin, you must tell me who the father is."

"I can't, Father. I just can't."

"Then leave the confessional, girl. Leave this church and don't come back until you're ready to ask for God's mercy."

For the next two weeks, he pondered what to do about the foolish, evil girl. This whole business did not bode well for him. What would the bishop say if he found out? Are you not able to control the people in your own parish? Just the week before, the cranky old man had summoned him and informed him that he was thinking of closing down his church in Ballyturan, citing, among other things, the expense of replacing the old, leaking roof. The bishop's words had stunned him. After twelve years as a priest, he'd finally gotten his own parish. Admittedly, a small church in a small village was not much. He'd hoped for an assignment in a big city like Limerick or Dublin. But what would become of him if his church was shut down and he lost his parish? Back to being an assistant curator? If this scandal reached the bishop's ears, for sure, all was lost...

Father Dunne was jarred out of his deep contemplation by the sound of a log falling out of the hearth. He pushed it back with a poker, refilled his glass, and sat back down and his mind slowly drifted back to the past again. That pregnancy business with Maeve Cafferty had been a difficult time for him. But then, thanks be to God, salvation had come to him in the form of John Twomey. It was almost two weeks after the girl's confession that Twomey, a grizzled, sour-faced farmer, came to see him.

"I'm not a man of many words," he said, sitting down across the desk from the priest, "so I'll get right to the point." Dunne nodded, wondering what this was all about. "You need a new roof for your church." It was more a statement than a question.

"Aye, I do."

"Well, I have a proposition for you. I'll pay for a new roof."

The priest was so dumbfounded by such good news that he'd missed the word "proposition." Before this moment, his impression of Twomey had not been a good one. He'd pegged him as a skinflint who contributed precious little to the collection basket. And if his sporadic attendance at Sunday Mass was any indication, he was a Catholic in name only. But perhaps God had shined a light into his dark soul.

The priest rubbed his hands together. "John Twomey, God and I will bless you for the rest of your days if you do this wonderful thing."

Twomey waved the priest off with a thick, calloused hand. "I said it was a proposition. I want something in return."

"Anything, John. I'll give you anything that's in my power to give."

"I want to marry Maeve Cafferty and I want you to arrange it."

The priest was struck speechless. The fool might as well have said he wanted to be put up for sainthood. What he was asking was beyond preposterous. "Are you daft altogether, man? For one thing she's more than twenty-five years your junior. And how in God's name could you possibly imagine that she would want to marry the likes of you?"

"Because she's pregnant and the man who did it to her will not marry her."

"And how do you know that?" the priest snapped.

"Ach, man, this is a small village. There are no secrets here."

That statement nettled the priest. Why was he the last man in the village to hear this bit of news? "Who is the father?"

"Barry McCartan."

That didn't surprise the priest. Didn't he see them every Sunday morning mooning at each other instead of paying attention to God's holy Mass? "How do you know he won't marry her?"

"Because he's run away. He's a deserter, that's what he is."

That did surprise him. Admittedly, he hadn't had much contact with the solitary young man. But he seemed to be a responsible soul, even if he was mixed up with the Easter Uprising and those firebrand Irish Volunteers.

"Why do you want to marry her?"

"I lost my wife almost ten years ago. It's hard being alone. I'm a man, and a man has needs…"

"Yes, yes, yes," Dunne waved him off. He didn't want to hear any more about John Twomey's needs. "But why this young girl? Why not marry the widow Mrs. Conlon? Or, even better, the widow Mrs. Brennan? Didn't she inherit a fine farm from her late husband and—"

Twomey made a face. "I don't want an old women in her forties."

"Well, so are you," the priest countered in exasperation.

Twomey pounded the desk. "It's Maeve Cafferty I want. And it's Maeve Cafferty I'll have or they'll be no roof for your church."

Ignoring the implied threat, the priest said, "I'll need time to think about your proposal."

Twomey stood up. "All right, but you haven't much time. I'll want to marry her before she has the baby. You make this happen and you'll have your new roof."

As soon as the farmer left, Dunne, with a shaking hand, poured himself a generous dram of Bushmills and sat down to consider the farmer's peculiar proposal. When he'd first heard Twomey's proposition, he did indeed think it was preposterous, but now that he thought about it, maybe it wasn't so absurd after all. A marriage between Maeve Cafferty and John Twomey would certainly solve a lot of problems for him—and, of course, for Maeve Cafferty. If they married, the bishop need never know about a pregnant unmarried girl in his parish. He would have a new roof over the church at no cost to the diocese. And that would be certain to put him in good stead with the bishop. The girl's reputation would not be sullied and John Twomey would have a wife. What did it matter that she was twenty-five years his junior? Didn't we all have to make sacrifices in life? Having convinced himself, he slammed the glass on the desk. "Sure it's the right thing to do," he said aloud. "The only thing to do. A marriage will be to everyone's benefit."

But how would he persuade the girl and her widowed mother? As he thought about it, it occurred to the shrewd priest that convincing the mother would be no problem. The woman had grown up in a time where it was unthinkable to question the wisdom of a priest. The girl, however, was another matter. Like so many young people nowadays, she was entirely too spirited and independent for his taste. She would be a challenge, but he was sure he would rise to the occasion.

The next day, he sent Nora off to fetch Mrs. Cafferty and her daughter. Now, as they sat across the desk from him, fearfully glancing about the room, he was beginning to have second thoughts. What right did he have to dictate to this young girl how she should live her life? But then he thought of the leaking roof. No, he was not dictating, he told himself firmly. He was only doing what was best for all concerned.

He looked at the two women seated in front of him. "Now then," he said, sternly. "About this business of… of…" his voice trailed off. He cleared his throat. "Maeve Cafferty, I put it to you: Will your Barry McCartan marry you?"

At the sound of his name, tears welled up in her eyes and she looked down at her lap where she was wringing a handkerchief between her hands. "He's gone," she said in a small voice.

"Gone? Gone where?"

"I don't know."

"So, the man who did this to you has abandoned you?" When she didn't answer, he slammed his hand on the desk, causing her to jump. "He has abandoned you, is that not right?"

She shook her head in dull defeat.

He turned his attention to the mother. "And so, Mrs. Cafferty, let me ask you. What is to be done now?"

The mother shrugged helplessly, overwhelmed by the whole situation. "I'm sure I don't know, Father."

"Well, I'm sure you realize that something must be done?"

The woman looked around the room, dazed. "I suppose, Father."

"Well, I do believe I have a solution," he said with as much confidence as he could muster.

At those words, the mother's expression became that of a drowning woman who has just been pulled from a raging sea. "Oh, thank you, Father. Thank you."

Maeve, on the other hand, continued to study the handkerchief twisting in her hands.

"It's clear she must be married," he announced matter-of-factly.

At those words, Maeve's wary eyes flicked up momentarily, but she quickly lowered them.

"But, who...?" the mother asked, now totally bewildered.

"I have just the man. John Twomey."

Maeve let out a cry and her hand went to her mouth. Now the tears did flow.

Mrs. Cafferty shook her head, struggling to digest what he'd just said. "John Twomey? Do you mean the same farmer who lives on the west road, Father?"

"Aye, the same." Dunne went on quickly, hoping to drown their doubts and protestations in a torrent of words. "I'm sure you'll agree, it'll be best all around. Maeve will salvage her reputation. The baby will not be a bastard. He will have a father. I must tell you that John Twomey is not without substantial capital, and he does have a fine, prosperous farm there. He will be able to provide handsomely for Maeve and the baby. He's a hard worker and furthermore—"

"No."

Dunne's narrowed eyes shot to Maeve. "What did you say?"

"No," she said in a low, but firm voice. "I will not marry that old man or any old man or any man for that matter that I don't choose."

This was exactly what he was afraid of. He'd thought she'd been beaten down, but apparently there was still some cheekiness left in her. He would have to put a stop to that attitude straight away. "That *you* don't choose?" he said with all the sarcasm he could muster. "Maeve Cafferty, you are in no position to choose anything—except disgrace, poverty, and ostracism from your church and your community."

The mother came to her daughter's defense. "But, Father... how can you ask her to marry a nasty, bitter man like John Twomey?"

He threw up his hands in frustration. "Do you know what the alternative is, Mrs. Cafferty? Do you?"

She shook her head, cowed by his overpowering voice.

"Have either of you ever heard of the Magdalene laundries?"

By the sudden, stricken expression on Mrs. Cafferty's face, she had, but not her daughter.

"Well, let me tell you about it. It's a place where fallen women— girls like you, Maeve Cafferty—go when they have a child out of wedlock. You'll be required to undertake hard physical labor, including laundry and needle work. You'll also endure a daily regime that includes long periods of prayer and enforced silence. Oh, and one more thing. Your baby will be taken from you and given to people who will provide the child with a decent, God-fearing upbringing."

"I won't go there," Maeve said bravely. "I'll get a job. I'm strong. I can work."

"Not in Ballyturan you'll not, my girl. No self-respecting Christian would hire someone such as the likes of yourself. So which will it be, Maeve Cafferty, a marriage to a decent God-fearing man or will it be the Magdalene laundries? You've no other choice."

Maeve Cafferty and John Twomey were married three weeks later in a quiet ceremony attended by only the priest, Nora, Maeve, her mother, and John Twomey.

Father Dunne, shaking the cobwebs of the past from his head, reached for his glass, but it was empty. Slowly he got up from his chair and knelt down by the side of his desk. Clasping his hands in prayer, he said, "Dear God, please forgive me. Please forgive me."

As he climbed the stairs to his bedroom, he took a modicum of comfort in knowing that at least no one else had seen that cursed letter. They had been consigned to the flames and the matter was closed for good and all

CHAPTER FIVE

The next day, after she'd finished her chores at the rectory, Cathleen, burning with excitement, rushed off to find her friend Claire. Not wishing to encounter Claire's stepfather, old man Twomey, a nasty, suspicious man, and someone to be avoided at all costs, Cathleen cautiously made her way across the fields to Claire's farm. With a sigh of relief, she spotted Twomey plowing a field at the far end of his property, stumbling and shuffling through a cloud of brown dirt as his horse doggedly plowed another furrow. Cathleen could never understand why he was the way he was. John Twomey was a fifth generation farmer in his late seventies. Why was he still farming at his age? The farm was small, but, as far as she could tell, it afforded him a decent living. Instead of being so crotchety he should have been grateful for a dutiful wife and daughter who had never given him a moment's grief.

She crept up to the back of the house, hoping to find Claire alone. She loved Claire's mother, a vibrant woman with a wonderful sense of humor, but Cathleen wasn't sure how she would react to what was in that letter. Best to give it to Claire first.

Fortunately, she found her friend alone, hanging sheets and pillow cases in the field behind the farmhouse. As a child, Claire had been a flaming redhead, but as she grew older, her hair darkened to rust-red. With her long, flowing hair, green eyes and fair complexion, the twenty-seven-year-old was the prize sought by every young man in the village and beyond. Cursed—or blessed, depending on to whom one spoke—with a stubborn, independent streak, she had turned down any number of suitors, much to the dismay of her mother and the fury of her stepfather.

Cathleen crept up behind her friend and tickled her ribs. Claire jumped in alarm. "For Jaysus' sake, what in the world's the matter with you? Sure you scared the living shite out of me."

"Ach, that's because you're always daydreaming," Cathleen said, leaning against a low stone wall. "Sure the devil himself could sneak up on you and steal your very soul and you none the wiser."

"I have a rich inner life," Claire said with a grin. "And everyone knows that the devil can't take the soul of someone with a rich inner life."

29

Cathleen took the letter out of her apron pocket. "I have something to show you, Claire, but I'm not sure I should."

"You sound daft, Cathleen Mullen. What are you talking about?"

Cathleen grew very serious. "Claire, what I'm about to show you must be kept a secret. Do you understand?"

"No, I don't. You're talking like a mad woman all together."

"I've stole something from Father Dunne's office."

Claire dropped her laundry basket. "For God's sake, what are you saying, Cathleen? That's a mortal sin."

"Claire, I had to. It concerns your father. You're real father." She handed the letter to her friend.

When an ashen-faced Claire finished reading it there were tears in her eyes. "So, my father is dead," she said dully.

"Are those tears for him that abandoned you and your mother all those years ago?" a puzzled Cathleen asked.

"I don't know. He's always been on my mind, I can tell you that. I used to torture myself with questions. Why did he leave us? Was it my fault? Would he ever come back? Whenever I'd see a stranger coming along the road into the village, my heart would race thinking it might be him." She looked at the letter again. "I have a half-brother."

"Aye, that you do. That's why I had to steal the letter. So you'd know. There were more copies of that letter. I think Father Dunne was supposed to give them to other people in the village, but he burned them all instead."

"And why would he do such a thing?"

"I have no idea. He's a peculiar one, that Father Dunne. So, are you gonna tell your mum?"

"I don't know."

"Are you gonna answer the letter?"

"I don't know. I'm just so confused. This is just... so... shocking." And the tears came.

Cathleen hugged her friend. "I know, I know. But remember, Claire Twomey, this must be our secret."

"Aye," she said, slipping the letter into her apron pocket. It will be our secret."

CHAPTER SIX

Yorkville
New York City

As he had been doing everyday for the past several weeks since he'd sent his letter, Matt checked the mailbox as soon as the mailman came, hoping to find a reply to his letters. But so far, nothing. Christmas and New Year's had come and gone and now it was April. After all this time, he concluded that his father had not come from the village and he would not be hearing from anyone there. He wasn't sure if he was disappointed—or relieved.

Right after the first of the year, he'd gone to work at the brewery, much to Neil's disgust and dismay. He explained to his friend that he wasn't looking for a career at this particular moment and the brewery job—a mindless, repetitious one on the bottling line—was just what he needed to keep his life simple. But even though the job was satisfyingly monotonous, he chafed at the drudgery of a nine-to-five job. And that lack of industriousness bothered him.

He'd always had a job, starting as a twelve-year-old shoeshine boy on 86th Street. Not wanting to have a job made him feel like a slacker, a bum. But at least he wasn't alone in thinking that. He'd become friends with several young veterans who hung out at the Emerald Isle and they all felt the same way he did. The consensus was that after the action and excitement of war, the prospects of returning to dreary, mundane jobs in factories or banks just wasn't very appealing. What they said sounded good, when he was drunk. But in the morning, when he sobered up, he realized it was nothing more than pure rationalization. Some of those men in the bar, with their self-serving opinions, were turning into alcoholics and that scared him. He was spending far too much time in bars, alternating between the Black Forest and the Emerald Isle. Still, he had to admit, it felt good. When you're drunk, there are no worries, no thinking. Just oblivion. Still, deep down, he knew he had to change his lifestyle and he would. Just not right now.

~~

Ballyturan

Spring came in early May. After a harsh, dreary winter of bone-chilling rain and relentless winds, the profusion of flowers in the meadows and the bright blue skies above were a welcome relief. But a fidgety Claire Twomey saw none of that. For the past half hour, she had been pacing back and forth outside the rectory waiting for Cathleen to be done with her chores. It was just after three when her friend came out.

"What are you doing here?" a surprised Cathleen asked.

A serious Claire took her arm. "Come on, let's go for a walk."

They took the meandering, quarter mile-long road that followed the sloping hills down to Dingle Bay. They came out on a wide, expansive beach patrolled by squadrons of screeching gulls, petrels, and terns, soaring and diving in their ceaseless quest for food. About a quarter of a mile east of them, a man was applying a fresh coat of tar to his overturned currach. From a distance, the hump-hulled black boat resembled a beached whale.

Cathleen elbowed Claire. "Uh, uh. There's queer old Hugh Cleary."

"Don't say that. He's a nice man."

"Everyone says he's tetched."

"Why? Is he crazy because he doesn't talk to anyone? I don't blame him. There are a lot of people in Ballyturan that I'd as soon not talk to as well."

"But he lives all alone in that little shack up on the hill. And why isn't he married? And why doesn't he have children?"

"Oh, and is that now a requirement for living, Cathleen Mullen? If so, then I must be tetched as well. For I do not plan to get married and I certainly do not intend to have children."

She waved to him. He looked up and waved back.

By the time they'd walked a mile down the beach in the opposite direction, they were completely alone. Claire stopped and faced her friend. "I've made up my mind," she announced. "I'm gonna write to him in America."

"Oh, my God. Are you sure?"

"Yes, I'm sure. Haven't I been thinking of nothing else since you gave me the letter?"

"Have you told your mum?"

"No, I have not."

"And why not?"

"Because she'd probably talk me out of it. I'm sure she has no interest in contacting a son of the man who abandoned her. And for sure old John wouldn't want any part of him either. The few times he's mentioned my real father, it was always with a great deal of spit and venom." In her stepfather's presence, she had to call him "Da", but out of his sight and hearing, she derisively referred to him as "old John."

"What will you say?"

"I don't know. That's why I wanted to talk to you. You're to help me write the letter."

"Sure I wouldn't know what to say. I've never written a letter in my life, never mind to a Yank in America."

"Well, neither have I, but together, we'll think of something."

"I think you're daft," she said, grinning. "But I'm game. When will we do it?"

"Right here and now." She took a package out of her handbag. "I went into Dingle and bought the stationery."

"You went all the way to Dingle? Are you balmy? I'm sure O'Neill's carries letter writing paraphernalia."

Claire plopped down on the sand. "I don't want the whole village to know what I'm about."

"Oh, that's true." Cathleen was starting to get excited about this adventure, but then she remembered dour old Father Dunne. "Oh, God, Claire. What if Father Dunne finds out about this? He'll know I stole the letter for sure."

"And how would he know that? You said, yourself, he burned all those letters. If he knew there was one missing, he'd have thought you the culprit straight away."

Cathleen bit her lip. "I guess that's true," she said with little conviction.

Claire tore open the stationery package and pulled out a piece of writing paper. "Right. How will I begin?"

Cathleen ran her fingers through her wind-tossed hair. "I don't know. How about 'dear sir'?"

Claire made a face. "It's my half-brother I'm writing to, not the President of the United States."

"All right then. How about 'dear Matthew'?"

Claire nodded thoughtfully. "I think that's a good beginning." She wrote, Dear Matthew. "Okay, what's next?"

For the next hour, the two young friends struggled to compose the letter. By the time they came up with the finished product, the sand around them was littered with balled up pieces of stationery.

"All right," Claire said. "I think we've got it." She read the letter:

May 6, 1946
Dear Matthew McCartan,

*I am in receipt of your letter of December 12, 1945.
As to your query, I can inform you with certainty that your
father was indeed born and raised in Ballyturan. That is
the good news. The bad news, I regret to inform you, is
that you father abandoned a pregnant woman, leaving her
to fend for herself under the most dreadful and
embarrassing conditions imaginable. Not to put too fine a
point on it, your father was an abandoner, a disreputable
person, a coward, and a good-for-nothing. But I don't
hold that against you. As a God-fearing woman, I believe,
as the Bible says, that the sins of the father should not be
visited upon the son. I trust that this letter will satisfy your
curiosity. If you have any further questions, you can write
me at the return address.*

    Sincerely, your half-sister,
    Claire Twomey

~~

Yorkville

    Matt had given up checking his mailbox every day. He'd written his letter back in December and now it was May. With each passing week and month, his initial eager anticipation had given way to disappointment. He couldn't understand why had no one from Ballyturan bothered to write him. Even if his father didn't come from the town, he'd assumed that at least one of them would have the courtesy to tell him.

    Not expecting anything, he opened the mailbox and was stunned to see a letter from Ireland. Unable to wait until he got back to his apartment, he sat down on the stairs and ripped open the envelope. He had to read the letter two more times before the import of what it said sunk in. His father had abandoned a pregnant girl—and he had a half-sister. Was that why the old man wanted nothing to do with Ireland? Was he ashamed to face the terrible thing he'd done to that young woman all those years ago?

    Back in his apartment, Matt sat down at the kitchen table and wrote:

    May 23, 1946
    Dear Claire,
    *Thank you for responding to my letter. I must say, I
was completely shocked and stunned by what you wrote. I
had no idea that my father had done that or that I had a
half-sister. On his behalf and mine, may I offer my
sincerest apology for his despicable behavior. I realize
that you probably know nothing about my father, but is*

your mother still living? And if so, do you think she would
be willing to tell me what she knows about him? You see,
my father and I did not talk very much. And because of
that, I knew very little about him, but I would like to learn
more. I realize that talking about my father might be too
painful for your mother and I will understand if she does
not want to talk about it. I will await your reply.
     Sincerely, your half-brother,
     Matt

~~

Ballyturan

John Twomey looked up from his plow to see Paddy the postman frantically waving to him from the road. As he walked toward him, Paddy pulled an envelope from his sack.
    What's that you've got, Paddy?"
    "'Tis a letter for your Claire. From America."
    "America? Sure she knows no one in America."
    "Be that as it may, but I have the letter here in me own hand."
    "Let me see that?"
    The postman frowned. "I don't know, John. It's addressed to Claire Twomey. I should deliver it to her meself."
    "Don't be daft, man. Am I not her own father?"
    "Aye, still…"
    "Do you really want to ride your bicycle all the way up that hill?"
    Paddy studied the steep hill and the uneven, rutted road. It was the end of a long day and he had a murderous thirst that could only be quenched by a quick pint of porter. "I guess it'll be all right," he said, handing the letter to the farmer.
    Making a big show of indifference, Twomey casually stuffed the letter into his overalls. "I'll see that she gets it," he called out as the postman rode away.
    He waited until the postman was out of sight before he took the envelope out. "Jaysus Christ…" he muttered when he saw the name on the return address. He tore the envelope open and his scowling face reddened as he read the letter.

~~

John Twomey barged into Father Dunne's study with Nora right behind him. "I couldn't stop him, Father. He pushed his way past me."
    Dunne saw the fury on the farmer's face and said, calmly, "That will be all, Nora. Thank you." He waited until she closed the door. "What's

the meaning of this Twomey?" he snapped. "Have you lost your senses all together?"

The farmer threw the letter on the desk. "You said we were done with him."

The priest read the letter and sat back in his chair, his face ashen. "I don't understand. How did she come to write him?"

"I'm sure I don't know. Do you?"

"No, no. Of course not." The old priest's mind was reeling. Could Claire have somehow seen a copy of the letter? No, that was impossible. Hadn't he burned all the letters himself?

"Well, what do we do about this?" Twomey demanded.

"You'll do nothing," the priest said, trying to remain unruffled. "Destroy the letter. When he doesn't hear back, he'll assume your wife wants nothing to do with him."

"You said that before. What if he writes again?"

"Then you'll see to it that she does not see another letter from that McCartan boy," Dunne said sternly. "Make some kind of arrangement with Paddy to ensure that he delivers all the mail to you directly. Anything that comes from America, destroy it."

~~

Father Dunne had done his best to sooth Twomey's anger, but he, too, was angry and he had serious fears about the motives of young McCartan. Now, sitting in Squire Kerrigan's library, he hoped Kerrigan would be able to assuage those fears.

Kerrigan poured two sherries and gave one to the priest. When he was seated behind his desk, he said, "How did young Claire find out about McCartan?"

Dunne took a sip of the sherry, giving him time to collect his thoughts. A whisky drinker his whole life, he knew nothing about fancy drinks like sherry, but he was quite certain that it was very expensive. Still, he'd have given anything for large dram of whisky. "I have no idea," he said, after a long pause.

Kerrigan continued to pin the old priest with an accusatory glare. "She mentioned the letter, the letter that you were supposed to have burned. How do you explain that?"

Dunne squirmed under the squire's biting tone. "I did burn them," he said in protest. "Every last one of them. There is no way..." His voice trailed off as he had a sudden flashback to that day. When he'd gotten back to his study, young Cathleen was there dusting the room. She had a look of guilt on her face, but that wasn't out of the ordinary. Most of the people in Ballyturan looked guilty when they spoke to him. But it was more than guilt. There was also a look of... fear. And, in that moment, it all came together.

"My God," he said, more to himself than to Kerrigan. "I think I know what happened. Cathleen Mullen comes in several times a week to help Nora with the house cleaning. And she's best friends with Claire Twomey. The letter was sitting there on my desk right out in the open. She must have read it and told Claire about it." The old priest's face reddened in anger at the cheek of a girl who would dare read his private correspondence. "Just wait till I get hold of that impertinent young girl. I'll—"

"Dunne, listen to me. You will not confront her about the letter."

"But—"

Kerrigan put up a hand to silence the priest. "The best way to deal with this letter business is to pretend that it never happened. The only ones who know about the letter are you, me, Heaney, Twomey, and perhaps Claire Twomey and the Mullen girl. If you start questioning her, it will only bring undue attention to this letter business and it will soon be all over the village."

"So you're saying that Twomey shouldn't confront his daughter to demand to know how she found out about McCartan?"

"That's exactly what I'm saying. Fortunately, Twomey was able to intercept this latest letter. When McCartan doesn't get an answer, he'll assume that Maeve doesn't want to talk to him."

Dunne gulped down his sherry and prayed to God that Kerrigan was right.

CHAPTER SEVEN

Yorkville

Since he'd gotten the letter from Claire Twomey, Matt resumed monitoring his mailbox with renewed anticipation. Everyday he checked the mailbox, hoping to find a letter from Ireland. Yet his anticipation was tinged with apprehension. What were the chances that the woman his father had abandoned would want anything to do with him? After a couple of months with no letter, his worst suspicions were confirmed and he gave up checking his mailbox. Obviously, she wanted nothing to do with him. He couldn't blame her, but he did wonder why Claire hadn't taken the time to write him about her mother's decision.

He forced himself to drop his crazy obsession with his father. It was time to admit that the only link to the old man's life was a woman in Ireland whom he had terribly wronged. In the end what did it matter who his father was? Besides, what did he expect to find? The little he did know was disappointing and shocking. Why should he continue this ridiculous and painful quest? In the end the only thing that really mattered was who he was.

Now that he'd put this fixation out of his head, he went to work every day and threw himself, as best he could, into the the monotonous task of making sure that every bottle that rattled by him on the bottling line was properly sealed. Occasionally, he thought about the GI Bill. He knew he should take advantage of that great opportunity to go to college, but he couldn't seem to get enthused enough to actually go talk to the administrators at City College. He was vaguely aware that an oppressive lethargy was beginning to seep into his life and that troubled him. More and more, he was seeing vets he'd met at the Emerald Isle becoming raging alcoholics and he didn't want that to happen to him. He would have to stop hanging out in bars, but not just yet.

~~

He was sitting at his usual spot at the bar late one evening, when Neil, with a stricken expression on his face, barged through the door. "Matt, did you hear about your friend, Barney Killeen?" He slapped a newspaper down on the bar in front of Matt. "It's all right here in the Journal American."

"I haven't seen a paper today. What happened?"

"He killed himself."

"What? How can that be? I was just talking to him right here yesterday. He seemed fine to me then."

"I don't know. All I know is the paper said he blew his brains out. His mother came home and found him lying in a pool of blood."

"Jesus Christ..."

Neil looked at his watch. "Jeez, I've gotta run. I'm having dinner with my boss and I can't be late. I might get a promotion tonight, if I don't spill soup all over my boss. Hey, I'll talk to you tomorrow."

Stunned by the news about Barney, Matt finished his beer, scooped up his change from the bar, and left. He knew the other guys who knew Barney would be coming in shortly and he was in no mood to talk to them about Barney's suicide. Besides, he was sure the news would become just another excuse for everyone getting stinking drunk.

On his way home, he stopped at a deli and picked up six pack. Sitting in his darkened living room with the six pack on the couch next to him, he opened a beer, took a swig, and tried not to think about his friend, Barney. But it was no use. The memories—what little there were—came. The word "friend," he decided, was a little strong. The truth was, he hadn't known Barney Killeen very long. In fact, they'd met in the Emerald Isle, shortly after he'd gotten back. There were a handful of guys just like them who hung out at the bar and he got to know them all. They had a lot in common. They were all recently discharged vets, lost and aimless, just trying to find themselves again after the hideous experience of war. Earlier, he had told Neil that Barney had seemed "fine." Now, he realized, that wasn't true. Barney had never been fine, at least since Matt had met him. He was always drunk—morning, noon, and night. Lately, he'd become more morose than usual. Did he ever use the word suicide? Matt couldn't recall that, but he did remember him always going on about the futility of life. Once in a while, he talked about packing it in. But by "packing it in," Matt assumed that he meant quitting his job at Gristedes. Now he realized it meant much more than that and he regretted missing the signals. Had he'd recognized the signs, could he have saved Barney from suicide? He told himself no, but, deep down, he had his doubts.

By the time he worked his way through the six pack, it was almost midnight. In spite of being slightly drunk—or maybe because of it—two verities of life suddenly became crystal clear to him. One, life was short. And two, only important things mattered. And in that moment of revelation, he came to an unexpected decision that stunned him—he would go to Ireland and try to find out for himself just who is father was and, by extension, who he was. Now that he'd made up his mind, it felt as though a great weight had been lifted off his shoulders. Finally, he had a purpose in life. A goal. A destination.

~~

The next morning, too excited to sleep, he was up at dawn to write a letter.

July 19, 1946
Dear Claire,
    I assume that because I didn't hear from you, your mother does not wish to speak to me about my father. I certainly understand her position. Still, I have so many unanswered questions that I feel I must come to Ireland to find answers to those questions for myself. I hope I will be able to meet with you while I am there.
    Sincerely, you half-brother,
    Matt

~~

Knowing that they would try to talk him out of it, Matt waited until he'd completed his travel plans before told his friends.

"Ireland?" Gus said, raising his bushy eyebrows in astonishment. "Why do you want to go to Ireland?"

Matt grinned. "It's a long story, Gus." It was a long story, which he'd tried to tell Gus several times. Gus would listen attentively, and then, he always asked the same question: "Yeah, but why do you want to go to Ireland?"

"You know, Mattie, you might not have a job when you get back," Gus warned.

Matt knew that. His supervisor had told him as much. "I guess I'll just have to take my chances."

His friend Neil tried a different tack: "You're no kid, Matt. You're twenty-two. You should be seriously thinking about starting a career and not gallivanting off to Ireland."

"Yeah, well, Neil, it's a long story."

~~

Ballyturan

John Twomey, sitting in the village pub, was into his second pint when Paddy stuck his head in the door. Squinting into the gloom, he spotted the old farmer and went directly to him.

"And why have you dragged me away from my fields to meet you here?" an irritated Twomey asked.

Paddy sat down next to him and looked around furtively, even though it was early afternoon and there was no one else in the pub, except the publican, who was busy in the back room. "I've another letter from America addressed to your Claire," he whispered.

Twomey muttered an oath. After all these months, he'd assumed that young McCartan had given up his search. So, it wasn't over. He put his hand out. "Give it here."

Paddy hesitated, and again, looked around furtively. "I believe we agreed on a certain sum, did we not?"

"Ach, man," Twomey said, impatiently. He slapped a shilling on the counter. "Now, give me the damn letter."

~~

Father Dunne, John Twomey, and Brian Heaney sat in Kerrigan's library, anxiously watching the squire read the letter. Presently, he looked up. "So, he's coming to Ballyturan."

"Aye," they all said in unison.

"I don't understand this man," a frustrated Father Dunne said. "He's received not one ounce of encouragement, but he's coming here all the same. What kind of man is this?"

"Never mind that," Twomey said. "The question is: What are we to do with him?"

Kerrigan shook his head. "No, the real question is: How much does he know?"

An agitated Heaney jumped up. "Sure, what could he know? Hasn't Twomey here intercepted all the letters?"

"How do we know that a letter has not gotten through to Claire or someone else in the village?" Kerrigan countered.

That question stunned them into silence.

"I could ask Claire," Twomey volunteered.

"You'll do no such thing," Kerrigan said, crossly. "There's no need to stir the pot." The squire went to the fireplace and warmed his hands. "There's only one thing to do," he said. "Obstruct him at every turn."

"And what do you mean by that?" Twomey asked.

"There are two people he'll want to see when he comes here. And that's the two people he's written to—Father Dunne here, and Claire Twomey. Father, you will give him no information when he comes to see you. You will tell him you didn't know Barry McCartan, period. And you have nothing more to say. Twomey, you'll be responsible for keeping this man from visiting your farm and talking to Claire or Maeve. If we deny him contact with your wife and daughter, then there is not much he'll be able to learn."

"And what about Hugh Cleary?" Twomey asked. "What if he..."

"I don't think we have too much to worry about him," Heaney said with a chuckle. "The man's been off his head for years."

"There's truth in that," Kerrigan said. "If Cleary says anything, we'll say he's as mad as a hatter and doesn't know what he's talking about."

In spite of Kerrigan's optimism, the three men left, feeling uneasy and anxious about the coming visit of young McCartan to their village. On a pretext that he needed to talk to the squire about a business matter, Heaney stayed behind.

"What's on your mind, Heaney?" Kerrigan asked when the others had gone.

"What else, Commandant? The McCartan boy."

Kerrigan, who was jabbing at a log in the hearth, spun and pointed the poker at him. "Don't call me that," he said sternly. "That's been over a long time ago."

"Is it, now, Comm... I mean, Squire? Well, it seems that business with Barry McCartan isn't over. And wasn't all the trouble with him during the uprising?"

"What are you driving at?"

Heaney, avoiding Kerrigan's steely glare, hitched up his trousers self-consciously. "I'm just saying, I failed to complete my mission against Barry McCartan, clever bastard that he was, but I can succeed with his son."

Kerrigan quietly put the poker down, looking suddenly older than his seventy-eight years. "They'll be no talk of that, Heaney. That was over thirty years ago and its best left in the past."

"But, Squire, the past is coming back..."

"That's enough. You're dismissed, Heaney."

"Yes, sir." Heaney saluted smartly and marched out of the study.

CHAPTER EIGHT

The squire, deep in thought, stepped through the French doors leading out to a fieldstone terrace overlooking a field where his extensive stable of horses were grazing. His favorite, Blathmac, named after a seventh century High King of Ireland, was a spirited black hunter. As he always did when released to the fields, he pranced about in a never-ending quest to impress the young fillies in the next field. In the past whenever Kerrigan was troubled or weighed down by the need to make a tough decision, a surefire remedy was to toss a saddle on Blathmac and ride the fields hard until both he and the horse were completely exhausted. But at the end of the ride, he'd usually made up his mind as to what had to be done. But he was too old for that sort of thing now. Crippled by arthritis, he hadn't ridden in years. So now, he had to content himself with sitting on the terrace and watching his horses instead.

As he settled onto a stone bench, Heaney's words echoed in his troubled mind—the past is coming back...

Thinking back to those days—and that damned Barry McCartan—he asked himself, yet again: How had it come to that? Part of the answer was obvious. The year of the uprising, 1916, was a turbulent time. What was it that the poet W. B. Yeats had said about the uprising? *All changed, changed utterly, a terrible beauty was born.* It was a time of hotheads and patriots, a time of Padraig Pearse, James Connolly, and Eoin MacNeill and so many other names of Irish freedom fighters that he'd half-forgotten over the years. It was a time of turmoil, but it was also a time of great excitement as well. After centuries of being under the oppressive yoke of English subjugation, freedom for Ireland seemed to be finally within reach.

The men of Ballyturan were not immune to the groundswell of nationalism and patriotism that swept the country. A brigade was quickly formed, consisting of two dozen men from Ballyturan—including John Twomey, Brian Heaney, Hugh Cleary, and Barry McCartan—as well as men from neighboring towns and villages. Because of his wealth and position, Kerrigan was appointed the commandant of the brigade.

Under orders, they made their way to Dublin. After a great deal of confusion and maddening indecisiveness, on Easter Monday, April 24th, the Volunteers, under the command of Pearse and Connolly, seized the

General Post Office. The next several days were a blur to Kerrigan. The British army fired cannon and shot into the Post Office day and night, killing and maiming hundreds of men. Finally, on Saturday, Pearse, realizing the hopelessness of the situation, surrendered. In the aftermath, Pearse, Connolly and thirteen others were executed. Kerrigan and most of his brigade were imprisoned. They were not released from jail until June of the following year, except for Kerrigan, who paid a huge bribe for his early release in March. It was shortly after their release that rumors began to circulate that young McCartan had informed on the Volunteers.

And he, Kerrigan, God forgive him, would soon use those rumors to eventually rid himself of the troublesome young man who had become a thorn in his side. Over the years, he'd absolved himself of his role in those terrible events by convincing himself that it wasn't his fault. It need not have been that way. If only that damn hotheaded fool, Barry McCartan, had been reasonable, everything would have turned out differently.

Water. It was all about something as simple as water.

The McCartans had a small farm adjacent to his. It wasn't much—a handful of acres, barely providing for the needs of McCartan and his only son. The wife had died years ago. But the farm did have one thing that Kerrigan's much larger farm did not have—and that was water. McCartan's farm was blessed with a large pond that was able to provide water for McCartan's handful of cows, as well as Kerrigan's large herd of cattle, horses, and sheep. For years, there had been an equitable arrangement between Kevin McCartan and himself. Kerrigan paid a yearly fee for unlimited use of the pond. The arrangement, as far as he was concerned, worked well for all concerned. But then the father died and his hot-headed son had to ruin everything.

Kerrigan's eyes drifted to a field in the distance. He could still remember standing on this very terrace all those years ago and seeing young Barry McCartan trudge across the field with a purposeful stride. He couldn't have been more than twenty at the time.

Kerrigan greeted him cordially enough. "Good morning, Barry."

McCartan stopped at the bottom of the terrace steps and nodded curtly. "And good morning to you, Squire. We have to talk."

"Oh, about what?"

"The arrangements over the water."

Kerrigan felt his stomach tighten. He'd been expecting, yet dreading, this moment. He just didn't think there would be a confrontation so soon, with the young man's father dead less than a week. It had been easy dealing with the senior McCartan, a mild-mannered man who was suitably intimidated by Kerrigan's money and power. It had been quite easy to talk the father into a financial arrangement that was favorable to himself.

Where the father was easygoing and agreeable, his son was hot-tempered and stubborn. He's seen young Barry in action many times on market day in the village. Whether buying or selling, he drove a hard bargain and had ruffled the feathers of more than a few farmers and tradesmen.

Kerrigan studied the young man at the foot of the steps, wondering how was the best way to approach him. "Well, I've had a suitable arrangement with your father all these years. I see no need to…"

"You cheated my da."

"Now, now," Kerrigan said, pointing his walking stick at the young man. "I don't like the tone of your voice. And I especially don't like your characterization of me as a cheat."

"But it's true all the same. I had no idea you paid my Da such a pittance for the rights to the water."

"Your father and I agreed it was a fair price."

"My Da only agreed because he was afraid of you. Well, I am not. I've talked to farmers up and down Dingle who have similar arrangements with the water. You've been grossly underpaying all these years."

Kerrigan was growing irritated with this vexing young man. "There is nothing further to discuss," he said, hoping to end this disquieting conversation.

"Squire Kerrigan, I'll tell you this. If you want to continue using my water, you'll have to pay a fair price. And that's my final word."

With a dismissive wave of his hand, Kerrigan turned on his heels and went into the house.

He thought he'd suitably intimidated the young McCartan, but the next morning, his lead stockman came rushing into the dining room where Kerrigan was having breakfast.

"Squire, there's a problem watering the stock."

"What is it, man?"

"That young McCartan won't let us bring the cattle onto his property."

"Pay no attention to that damn fool. Just drive the cattle to the pond."

"I can't, sir. He's got a shotgun and he's threatening to shoot any man who steps foot on his land."

Kerrigan threw his napkin down. "Well, we'll just see about that."

When he rode up to the gate, McCartan was still standing there, cradling a shotgun.

"What's the meaning of this, McCartan?"

"I'm just protecting my property from trespassers."

"What are you talking about, man? My animals have been crossing on to your property for years."

"Well, there'll be no more of that. Not until we make a new arrangement about the water."

"Damn it, man. I already have an arrangement. With your father. We shook hands on it."

"Well, that hand is dead, isn't it? And you'll not shake my hand on such a bad bargain."

There followed long and protracted negotiations over the next several days. In desperation, Kerrigan even offered to buy the farm, but McCartan refused his offer. Finally, when he realized he had no choice—his animals were in dire need of water—he agreed to a new price that was five times what he'd been paying previously. It wasn't so much the money—he could easily afford the higher fee. What galled him was that he'd been bested by an ignorant farmer—and a young callow one at that. And to add insult to injury, young McCartan would not, in the time honored custom of Ballyturan, shake hands on the deal. He insisted on having a solicitor draw up a proper contract requiring signatures and witnesses. Kerrigan was painfully aware that word of these goings on had spread up and down Dingle. And now, every time he saw a cluster of men laughing, he imagined they were laughing at him.

After that public humiliation, Kerrigan vowed he would get his revenge on Barry McCartan. And that opportunity came shortly after he and the other members of the brigade were released from prison. All the time he'd been wallowing in the English jail, he'd been ruminating on how to get his revenge. It was Brian Heaney who gave him the answer.

One morning after Sunday services, Heaney approached Kerrigan as he was about to mount his horse. "Begging your pardon, Commandant," he whispered. "If I could have a word with you."

Kerrigan led his horse to a corner of the courtyard, away from the other parishioners. "Well, what is it?"

"I'm supposing you've been hearing the rumors about Barry McCartan?"

"I have."

"Well, as the Commandant of our brigade, shouldn't you order an investigation? Shouldn't there be a trial of some sort? And shouldn't there be some kind of proper punishment for him, traitor that he is?"

"Heaney, it is not your place to question your superior officer."

"Yes, sir. I understand that. It's just..."

"That will be all. I'll take it under advisement."

Initially, Kerrigan dismissed the quarrelsome Heaney's suggestion. He'd heard that there was bad blood between Heaney and McCartan, although he didn't know why. No doubt that was Heaney's motive for speaking out against McCartan. In any event, it was a moot point. Kerrigan was finished with the Irish Volunteers. After the debacle of the Easter Uprising, his initial patriotic fervor had waned. All those long, tedious months in prison had convinced him that it was futile to lead an armed insurrection against the might of the British Empire. A pragmatic man, he came to the conclusion that if they were to be successful, they would have to do it through diplomacy and negotiations. And that was beyond his purview.

Still, over the next several days, despite his dismissing Heaney's suggestion, the man's words kept coming back to him—shouldn't there be some kind of proper punishment... And those words struck a chord with him. He craved more than anything a chance to exact some kind of punishment against the troublesome McCartan. But what would it be? And how would he accomplish it?

One thing was certain: The present arrangement with McCartan was intolerable. He'd been forced to sign a one year contract. What if McCartan decided to charge him more for the water rights? What if he simply denied him water rights after the annual contract expired? The water arrangement was a sword of Damocles hanging over his head and he would have to do something about that.

A week later, Kerrigan met Heaney again on market day. Kerrigan had just sold him two cows. As the squire's stockmen loaded the cows into Heaney's cart, Heaney pulled Kerrigan aside. "Commandant, have you given any consideration to what we spoke about last Sunday?"

"I have. There's no point. What good would an investigation be? There are no witnesses to testify to McCartan's treachery."

"Ah, but you're wrong there, Commandant. There is a witness."

"Who."

Heaney looked around furtively. "Me."

"What are you talking about man?"

"When we were in the jail, didn't I overhear him talking to the guards? I was in the next cell. In the beginning, they just passed the time of day, you know, where are you from and that sort of thing. But then they began plying him with cigarettes and the like. And then, one night, a British officer came to his cell. I was able to hear the whole conversation. He told the man everything, Commandant. He gave up the names of all the Volunteer lads who weren't in the Post Office with us. He told them where our weapons were stockpiled. I heard it all with my own two ears, I did."

"Why didn't you come forward with this information immediately?" Kerrigan asked sharply.

"Sure I thought there'd be an investigation, sir. Maybe a trial. I was prepared to come forward. But there was no trial, and that's why I came to you, Commandant."

Kerrigan struggled to contain his elation. This could be exactly what he needed to rid himself of McCartan. If he was convicted by a tribunal, the sentence for an informer was death. He felt a momentary stab of guilt. It was true that he desperately wanted to be rid of McCartan, but, good God, he didn't want him dead. But he quickly assuaged his conscience with a comforting thought: If what Heaney had just said was true, then McCartan was a traitor to the cause. And in that case, he did deserve to die. In any event, it would not be up to him. It would be up to the tribunal that he would convene to try McCartan.

The following week, he called a secret meeting of five senior officers in the brigade to hear the charges. None of the officers, with the exception of Kerrigan, came from Ballyturan and so none of them knew McCartan personally. Heaney was the only witness, but a forceful one. Later, during deliberations, in support of Heaney's testimony, one senior officer pointed out that the British army had in fact swept through the Dingle after the Easter Uprising, arresting men and boys who were secret members of the Volunteers. At the time, everyone had wondered how they had discovered the identities of these men. Another officer pointed out that the British army had raided several farms in his district where caches of weapons were stored. That could only have happened if someone had informed.

It took the court less than a hour to come to a verdict. Barry McCartan was found guilty of treason and sentenced to death.

Within the organizational structure of the Irish Volunteers there was a special group known as the "Squad," an assassination unit based in Dublin tasked with killing police officers involved in intelligence work. But they were also called upon from time to time to assassinate informers and turncoats within their own ranks. It was agreed that three men from Dublin would be assigned to assassinate Barry McCartan. It was also agreed that Brian Heaney would be added to the group because he was the only one who would be able to identify McCartan.

Liam Kerrigan left the secret trial, satisfied that he would soon be rid of Barry McCartan.

But nothing, he would soon learn, was that simple.

CHAPTER NINE

As Squire Kerrigan was reliving the past, Brian Heaney trudged down the hill from the squire's home in a heavy drizzle. Pulling his collar up and stuffing his hands in his pockets, he began to rehash the conversation he'd just had with the squire and his initial bravado began to wane. It occurred to him that he shouldn't have volunteered to take care of young McCartan. In fact, now he regretted even bringing the matter up in the first place. Perhaps the squire was right. It was a long time ago and maybe it was best that it all be left in the past.

The rain was coming down harder, but he hardly noticed because his mind had drifted back to those days—and the trial. Never in his life had he been under such pressure. Sitting there, facing those five grim-faced judges, he was almost sorry he'd agreed to testify against McCartan. It took everything in him to concentrate on the difficult questions they fired at him. What did you see? When did you see it? Who said what to whom? Who else overheard these conversations? He was a simple man, at the time just a butcher's apprentice in a small village. What did he know of evidence and hearsay and proper testimony and all those other words and phrases they threw at him, all of which he had precious little understanding? Still, he did his best to answer every question put to him, even if they had to ask the same question more than once and in different ways. In the end, he must have done good. Didn't they convict Barry McCartan of treason? And wasn't it on his testimony alone? To suppress the guilt that welled up in him that day and all the years since, he uttered the mantra that he had been reciting since the trial all those years ago. "I did the right thing… I did the right thing…"

"When the time comes," the squire had told him gravely, "you will go with the assassination team to carry out the sentence." The squire's pronouncement taken him aback. He'd hoped that after his testimony he could put the whole wretched business behind him. He'd joined the Volunteers because he craved action. They had given him training, and they had given him a rifle, but he never got to fire a shot in anger. For the entire five days the British fired shell after shell into the Post Office, he'd cringed under a desk, too terrified to move, let alone shoot back. He'd been ashamed of his behavior, but now he would have a chance to redeem himself.

One night, a week after the trial, he was summoned to a meeting at an abandoned farm a few miles outside Ballyturan. Waiting for him was the commandant, and three rough looking men from Dublin. The leader of the trio, a man named Kelly, scowled at Heaney when he came into the barn, but said nothing. He turned to Kerrigan, "Our information is that McCartan went to Dingle this morning on business. He'll becoming back on the West Road sometime tonight. We'll intercept him at the crossroads near Brandon Rock." He looked at Heaney. "Your job is to identify the man. Can you do that?"

Heaney was startled by the question. "Do you mean, now? Tonight?"

"Aye, tonight. Is that a problem?"

"No… no, it's just that I didn't think anything would happen tonight, that's all."

"Can you identify the man?" Kelly repeated.

"Of course," Heaney said, trying to sound brave. "Haven't I known him my whole life?"

"Right. Let's be on our way then."

"Gook luck," was all Kerrigan said as the four men set out for the crossroads.

~~

The Dublin men made Heaney nervous. They said little, and what little they did say, they said to each other. When they got to the crossroads, Kelly, with a minimum of conversation, directed the two men to set up on the other side of the road. Kelly and Heaney took up watch opposite them. As they sat crouched in the darkness, Heaney began to have second thoughts about what they were about to do. They were going to assassinate a man tonight. And not just any man, but—Barry McCartan, a man he knew. A man who was convicted on his sole testimony. And now he was here to identify him.

He felt his mouth go dry and he had a sharp pain in his stomach. He feared he was going to be physically ill. The story of Judas flashed in his mind and he recalled the accusing words of the priest in the pulpit, bellowing, "He betrayed our Lord for thirty pieces of silver. Who among you would do the same?"

Kelly touched his arm, causing Heaney to jump. "Someone's coming," he whispered, drawing a pistol.

Heaney strained to listen and soon heard muffled talking. Voices? McCartan was not alone. That meant there would be witnesses. What would be done with them? There was no mention of anyone else being with McCartan. Oh, Jaysus... This was all bollixed. Even thought it was a cool night, Heaney's face was drenched with sweat. He felt an uncontrollable urge to bolt from the bushes, run all the way home, and dive into his bed and wish that none of this had ever happened. But the presence of the armed and dangerous Kelly crouching beside him, made that impossible. He was certain the man would shoot him in the back if he tried to run. As the voices drew nearer, the full moon broke out from behind scudding black clouds. Heaney could clearly make out three men. Beside him, Kelly uttered an oath and signaled to the men across the road, holding up three fingers.

"Which one is McCartan?" Kelly whispered.

Heaney licked his dry lips, squinted, and wiped the sweat from his forehead with a sleeve. Even in the light of the full moon, it was difficult to make out the faces from that distance. But then, as they drew nearer, he recognized them—Jimmy Beggs, Hugh Cleary, and Barry McCartan.

Kelly tugged on Heaney's sleeve. "Which one is McCartan?" he hissed, an urgency in his voice.

"The one..." Heaney swallowed hard, "the one to the right..."

Just as the three men were almost abreast of them, Kelly gave a signal to his two comrades across the road. They jumped out of the bushes and stood in the middle of the road, pointing their pistols at them. "Halt, right there."

In the next instant everything happened so fast that Heaney would never be able to recall the exact sequence of events. All he remembered was a terrifying and confusing kaleidoscope of disjointed images—the two Dublin men stepping into the road, pointing their pistols at the trio... McCartan pulling a pistol from his belt... Jimmy Beggs brandishing another pistol ... and Hugh Cleary with yet another pistol... the air erupting with the sound of gunfire... one of the Dublin men going down... then McCartan spinning and falling... Kelly rising from the bushes, firing a shot and going down in a hail of bullets... the air alive with the smell of gunpowder and fear... screams and shouts of men...

In a panic, Heaney snatched up Kelly's pistol which had landed at his feet. He turned and plunged into the brush, running for his life. Afraid to use the road, he raced through the woods. Thorns from briar bushes ripped his clothing and low-lying branches smacked him in the face, but he kept going. Finally, he could run no more. He stumbled, fell to his knees, and vomited and vomited until there was nothing left. Then, in the utter stillness, he heard the snap of a twig not far off. Oh, God, someone is following me. Quietly, he rose to his feet and, trying to be as silent as he could, he quickened his pace. But the sounds behind him dogged him. Someone was definitely coming after him. But who? He immediately thought of Kelly. The man was a professional assassin. But it couldn't be him. Wasn't he dead? Didn't he see it with his own eyes? But maybe he wasn't dead. Maybe he was just wounded. Heaney suddenly realized now, too late, that they would want no witnesses to their crime. Kelly—or one of the Dublin men—was coming for him.

Gasping for breath, he realized he could go no farther. He would have to stand and confront whoever was after him. He stepped behind a large oak. Wiping his sweaty palms, he pulled the pistol from his belt. He'd never fired a pistol in his life and he wasn't sure he knew how. Pressed up against the tree, he listened to the sounds coming closer and closer. When he judged the man was close enough, he spun away from the tree, aimed at the shadowy figure, closed his eyes, and squeezed the trigger in rapid succession. The loud report and brightly flashing muzzle stunned him. He didn't realize he was out of bullets until he heard the dull click, click of the hammer on an empty chamber.

Standing rigidly still, he continued to point the empty pistol at the body on the ground, not knowing what he'd do if it moved. But, it didn't move. A sense of elation overcame his terror when he realized he'd done it. He'd killed his stalker. Then a wave of nausea overcame him and, once again, he fell to his knees and vomited.

Wiping his mouth with his sleeve, he cautiously approached the body. He flipped him over and—"Jaysus, Mary, and Saint Joseph—It's Jimmy Beggs…!"

A crack of thunder over his head brought him back to the present. Dark storm clouds were forming over Dingle Bay and jagged cracks of lightening flashed across the sky. Tucking his head into his collar, Heaney sprinted toward home.

CHAPTER TEN

Ballyturan

Matt stiffly stepped off the bus, fatigued and travel-weary. After a week of a stomach-churning transatlantic voyage from New York City to Belfast, a cross-country bus trip to Limerick, and a switch to a local bus connection, he was finally here. Well, almost. The bus came no nearer to Ballyturan than the town of Dingle, almost four miles from the village.

It had been raining nonstop since early this morning, but now the clouds had given way to what he would soon learn was considered a reasonably sunny day on the Dingle Peninsula. In spite of his exhaustion, he welcomed the four-mile trek to Ballyturan. It gave him a chance to exercise his atrophied muscles and recalibrate his brain from the insane chaos of New York City to the tranquil, almost fairylike enchantment of Ireland's countryside. During the war, he had trudged through similar rural areas in France, Belgium, and Germany—with one major difference. Here there were no dead, bloated cows scattered along the roadside, no crumbling, artillery-ravaged homes, no streams of terrified refugees lining the roads, and—best of all—absent was the pervasive and sickening smell of death.

Approaching the outskirts of Ballyturan, Matt stopped, suddenly overcome by the simple beauty of the scene. So this is where his father had been born and raised. How many times, he wondered, had his father walked this very road? His eyes swept the hills and fields around him, a sight that his father would have seen daily. He was surprised at the deep emotion that filled him.

The tiny village was situated on a gentle sloping hill, starting at foothill mountains to the north and gradually sloping down to the shores of Dingle Bay. Dotting the surrounding hillside were a handful of white-washed cottages, plowed fields neatly divided by a jigsaw pattern of stone walls, and in the meadows, clusters of cows and grazing sheep.

As he came into the village, he saw that it was nothing more than a narrow street with a collection of small shops lining both sides. Halfway down the street was the Kerrigan Arms, at three stories the tallest building in the village. The bus driver had recommended it, adding with an impish grin that it was the only hotel in Ballyturan.

Farther down the street, he passed a small pub, a general store, and a butcher shop. He read the sign over the door: Meat Purveyor, Brian Heaney, Proprietor. Peering into the shop window, he saw a thickset man behind the counter chopping meat with the mindless ferocity of a man vanquishing an ancient enemy. Then the man did something odd. He looked up, spotted Matt, and with a sudden, startled expression, bolted into a back room.

At the far end of the street, on the crest of a hill, he saw the church, presumably the one to which he had written his letters. He retraced his steps and went into the Kerrigan Arms. There was no lobby to speak of, just an open room with a counter behind which was an attractive young woman engrossed a thick textbook. She had long blonde hair, which she now brushed away from her face, revealing inquisitive blue eyes.

"Hey, how're you doing?" she asked in a distinctive New York accent. When he didn't answer, she cocked her head and gave him a dazzling smile. "I know what you're thinking: Funny, she don't look Irish. Am I right?"

"Well... to tell you the truth, I didn't expect to hear anyone here with a New York accent."

"Brooklyn. Greenpoint, to be more specific. You?"

"Yorkville."

"Ah, German town. Funny, you don't look German."

"Actually, I'm Irish..."

"I was just joshing you. Of course you're Irish. You've got the map of Ireland all over your face."

"Oh, yeah... I suppose..." He found himself tongue-tied in the presence of this lovely young woman. "Um... do you work here?"

"Yep. I'm desk clerk, bartender, and chief bottle washer around here. Let me guess. You want to check in."

"Um, yeah. You have a room?"

"I got eight of them and they're all available," she said, sliding a pen and the hotel register toward him. "Things are slow right now. Fill that out."

When he'd finished, she read the entry. "Matthew McCartan. What brings you to Ballyturan, Matthew McCartan?"

"My father came from here."

"Ah, on a quest to seek out your ancestral roots?"

"It's a long story."

"Sounds mysterious." She handed him a key. "Room four, top of the stairs."

The room was small with just enough space for a single bed, a night stand, a dresser, and a chair. But that was all he needed. He stretched out on the soft bed, planning to taking a nap after his long bus trip. But his mind was racing with so many thoughts that he couldn't fall asleep. Ten minutes later, he came back downstairs.

She was still reading the same book. She looked up and grinned. "The call of the ancestors has disturbed your slumber?"

"I think I'm too tired to sleep. Do you know... excuse me, what's your name?"

"Karina."

"Karina, do you know the name of the pastor in the church up the street?"

"That would be one Father Aloysius Dunne, scourge of the young and godless teenagers in Ballyturan."

"Would you happen to know how long he's been the pastor here?"

"People say he's been here forever." Then she added with a grin, "Or maybe it just feels that way to them. If you want to go to confession, you'll have wait till Saturday."

Matt grinned. "Nothing all that serious. I just want to have a talk with him."

~~

Matt knocked on the red painted door of the rectory. An old woman with gray hair tied up in a bun opened the door and, when she saw him, her eyes widened in shock. "Glory be to God..."

Recalling the odd reaction from the man in the butcher shop, Matt was beginning to wonder if everyone in Ballyturan reacted this way to strangers.

"Hello, my name is..."

"And don't I know your name? And aren't you the spittin' image of your own father?"

"You knew my father?" Matt couldn't believe his luck. She was just the second person he'd spoken to in Ballyturan and she knew his father. Maybe his search wasn't going to be as difficult as he thought it would be.

"Aye, that I did, but I'll say no more about that," she said with a firm nod of the head.

He thought her response odd, but he let it go. "I'd like to see Father Dunne, if he's in."

"He's in all right, though I don't know if he'll want to see you."

Before Matt could ask her what she meant by that, she'd already disappeared down a hallway.

Nora slipped into the study where Father Dunne was working on his Sunday sermon. "He's here," she announced.

The priest looked up, not pleased with the intrusion. "Who's here?"

"Barry McCartan's son."

Dunne took off his reading glasses and threw them on the desk. "Good God. Do you mean here? Right here in my own rectory?"

"I do."

"Tell him I'm not here."

"I already told him you were here."

He put his head in his hands. "In the name of God, woman, then just find a way to get rid of him."

The stubborn old woman folded her arms. "You've got to see him sometime. You can't put him off forever."

He saw there was no point in arguing with her further. Besides, she was right. He couldn't avoid him forever. "Oh, all right. Show him in. But mind, you tell him I'm a very busy man."

She came back to Matt grim and all business. "Come with me. The Father will see you. But he's a very busy man."

She opened the study door and motioned him to go inside. Father Dunne, sitting behind his desk in his study, peered suspiciously at Matt over his reading glasses. "Yes, yes, what can I do for you?" he asked, impatiently.

Matt was surprised the priest didn't ask him to sit down. "I'm Matt McCartan, Father. I wrote a letter to you back in December asking if you..."

"Letter? What letter? I don't recall any letter."

Matt was beginning to think that the people of Ballyturan were a peculiar bunch. How many letters could a country parish priest receive from the states? And how many of those letters would contain such a detailed request? "In my letter," he said, patiently, "I was inquiring about my father, Barry McCartan. Don't you remember? I asked you to distribute additional copies of the letter to anyone in the village who might have known him."

"Ach, man, I get mail all the time. I can't be expected to remember every letter I get."

His protests rang hollow to Matt. For some reason, the priest was being hostile and evasive.

"So are you saying you never received my letter?"

"I'm saying, maybe I did and maybe I didn't. And I'll leave it at that."

Matt fought to control a compulsion to snap at the old fool. Instead, he said, "Did you know my father?"

"What did you say his name was?"

"Barry. Barry McCartan."

"Can't say that I did."

"Father, you would have been his parish priest. This is not a big village. How could you not remember one of your own parishioners?" Despite his best efforts, a tone of anger was creeping into his voice.

"And when was all that?"

"Around nineteen sixteen."

"Ah, well, there you have it. I was the pastor for only a few years at that time. Sure there were any number of people I didn't know then."

Realizing he was wasting his time with the priest, Matt started for the door. "Thanks for you help."

"Why are you doing this?" the priest called out.

"Doing what?"

"Dragging up the past, man. Digging into people's lives."

"I'm not interested in people, just my father."

The priest pointed a bony finger at Matt. "Nineteen sixteen was the time of the uprising. A bad time that. A lot of men did things that they were not proud of. You've no right poking into people's lives. For the love of God, man, let the dead bury the dead."

"Thanks for your advice," Matt said, slamming the door behind him.

~~

By the time Matt got back to the hotel, he'd calmed down from his prickly meeting with the old parish priest. Karina was still engrossed in the same book. "Is there someplace to get a drink around here?" he asked in exasperation.

She slammed the book. "You're in luck. I'm the bartender and I declare the bar open."

The entrance to the "bar" was off the dining room. As bars went, it wasn't much. Certainly nothing like the elaborate faux-Irish pubs in New York City. There was room at the bar for no more than four people, and there was just a handful of tables scattered about.

She saw the look of dismay on his face. "Take a good look, Matt. This is what a real Irish pub looks like. Well, actually, it's a bit smaller than your average pub, but that's because it's part of the hotel. Only guests use it. The locals drink at Kerrigan's pub down the street."

"Is that the same Kerrigan who owns this place?"

"The same. Liam Kerrigan owns most of everything in Ballyturan. What'll you have?"

"I don't suppose you have beer on tap"

"Just Guinness stout." When he made a face, she added, "It's an acquired taste."

"That's all right. I need something stronger anyway."

"Irish whisky is just the thing. Paddy's or Bushmills?"

"I don't know. Bushmills I guess."

She poured the whisky into his glass. "You have ice?" he asked.

"Ah, you Yanks," she said in a good imitation of a brogue, "everything has to be bitter cold with you. Now I ask you, why would you want to freeze the life out of a perfectly fine Irish whisky?"

"You have no ice."

"Correct. I gave up making it. No one, with the exception of the occasional crazy American, asks for it."

She poured the whisky. He smelled it and took a sip. "Taste's a little like scotch."

"Oh, lord, don't let an Irishman hear you say that. It's a gross insult to the 'water of life'."

"I'll try to remember that. What's that intimidating book I see you so engrossed in?"

"Just a little light reading – Language Universals and Linguistic Typology: Syntax and Morphology".

"Oh, my God. Why?"

"I'm a graduate student in historical linguistics at New York University. I'm here on a six-month grant to study Irish speakers. There are a ton of them right here on the Dingle Peninsula."

"I didn't think anyone spoke Gaelic anymore."

"A common misconception. The truth is, there are parts of Ireland where Irish is still spoken as a traditional native language and used daily. These regions are known individually and collectively as the Gaeltacht."

"So, why are you working here?"

"These grants don't pay much. I do this to supplement my expenses. Otherwise I'd be living under a bridge with the other trolls. Liam gives me free room and board."

"Liam?"

"Liam Kerrigan."

"Well, at least that's something. Karina... What kind of name is that?"

"Polish. Karina Jaworski from Greenpoint."

"I'm sure there's a long story about how a Polish girl ended up studying the Irish language?"

"Not too long. My mother's Irish."

"Ah, I see. Do you know Father Dunne?"

"By sight. I don't go to church. I'm a recovering Catholic, much to my mother's great despair. From what I have seen of him, he seems like a pretty cantankerous old buzzard."

"That was my opinion, too."

"Why did you go see him?"

"It's a long story, but the short version is I wrote him a letter last December. I explained that my father had just died and I thought he might have come from Ballyturan. I also enclosed a dozen copies and asked him to pass them on to anyone who might have known my dad."

"So, did he?"

"Not only didn't he pass on the letters, he claimed that he never received them in the first place. When I spoke to him, he was very evasive—almost antagonistic. I don't get it. What's the matter with that guy?"

"Have you ever heard of 'island mentality'?"

"No."

"It's a psychological state of mind, usually found in people living on isolated islands. But it's not exclusive to people living on an actual island. People living in any isolated area, such as Ballyturan, develop their own mores and belief systems, which they think are far superior to anyone else's—especially strangers. The result is narrow-minded, ignorant, and hostile people."

"I think I just met one."

"Believe me, he ain't the only one. Don't get me wrong. There are a lot of very lovely people living here, but there are the 'others'."

Matt downed his whisky and shook his head in dismay. "The old priest was my best lead. I don't know what to do next."

"There's something I don't understand. If you didn't get a response from Father Dunne, how come you're here?"

"In early May, I got a letter from a young woman named Claire Twomey. She claimed she was my half-sister."

"Claire!"

"You know her?"

"Sure I do. She's wonderful gal with a great sense of humor. We've gone to a couple of dances in Dingle. She's your half-sister?"

"That's what she says."

"Well, then, why don't you go see her?"

Matt frowned. "To tell you the truth, I'm kind of embarrassed to see her. My father abandoned her mother when she was pregnant."

"Well, he might have been a bastard, but doesn't the Bible say something about not visiting the iniquity of the fathers on the children?"

"That's pretty much what she said in her letter."

"Well, there you go."

"Maybe you're right. Do you know where the Twomey farm is?"

"I pass it all the time when I go visit one of my old Gaelic speakers. It's about a mile east on the West Road. You can't miss it."

CHAPTER ELEVEN

After another whisky to fortify him, Matt set out for the Twomey farm. It wasn't as easy as she made it out to be. He passed a dozen or so farms, one looking very much like the other, but it was impossible to tell which one was Twomey's. It wasn't as though there was a sign that said: Twomey Farm.

Just as he was about to turn back in frustration, he saw a man on a bicycle coming toward him. With a large leather pouch over his shoulder and a black cap, he had the vague look of someone official.

"Excuse me," he said as the bicyclist came alone side, "can you tell me where the Twomey farm is?"

Paddy jumped off his bicycle. "And why not? Haven't I been delivering mail to John Twomey these past two years?"

Matt nodded tactfully, wondering why everyone in Ireland answered a question with a question.

"You're a Yank, aren't you?"

"Yes, I am."

"Are you the one who wrote that great big letter to Father Dunne?"

The question startled Matt. So the old priest had received his letter. But why would he lie about it? "Yes, I did."

"I thought so. Let's see, Twomey's farm," he said scratching his chin. "Why it's just down the road a wee bit. You'll find it on the right side of the road. You'll see himself plowing the field."

Matt thanked the man, and continued on his way. "A wee bit" turned out to be a couple of miles. Finally, up ahead, he saw a man who looked to be in his late seventies plowing a field.

Matt called out from the road. "Excuse me..."

Twomey looked up and his fixed scowl quickly turned to a look of startled amazement. Matt didn't know what to make of these people. First the butcher, then the priest's housekeeper, and now Twomey. What was it about him that startled everyone?

"What is it you want?" Twomey asked gruffly.

"Are you Mr. Twomey?"

"I am."

"I believe you have a daughter, Claire. I'd like to speak to her."

"That's out of the question."

Matt's heart sunk. Could he have come this far only to find that she had moved away? "Is she not here?"

"Of course she's here. Where else would she be?"

Matt felt the anger rising in him. Why in God's name was it so hard to get a straight answer out of these people? "OK. Then I'd like to speak to her."

"Didn't I just say you couldn't?"

"Yeah, but I don't understand. Why not?"

"Because I said so. And that's my final word on the subject." And with that he snapped the reins and his tired horse lunged forward.

Matt stood there in amazement. What the hell was going on? Why didn't anyone want to talk to him?

~~

Back at the hotel, an irate Matt recounted his frustrating encounter with Twomey to Karina.

"Island mentality," she said, pouring him a whisky. "It's island mentality, I tell ya."

"It's gotta be more than that. I feel like I'm being stonewalled."

"Why would they stonewall you?"

"I have no idea."

"Let's look at this logically. Obviously your father didn't owe anyone money. Otherwise they'd be banging the door down to collect from the rich Yank."

"Yeah, so?"

"So, maybe some of these people owe your father money and they think you're here to collect the debt."

"Well, I hear what you're saying, but as far as I know, no one owed my dad anything."

"Then that leaves land. The folks around here are real touchy about real estate. Did your father own a farm in Ballyturan?"

"I have no idea. Why?"

"The Irish have been known to feud over land for generations. If your father, or his father, owned land, that could be a reason why everyone is shunning you. They'd be afraid that you were here to reclaim your ancestral estate."

"I'm afraid there's nothing as grandiose as all that in the McCartan clan. At least I don't think so," he added, once again regretting that his father never spoke about his life in Ireland. If he had, maybe all of this would make sense.

He swirled the whisky in his glass. "I don't get it, Karina. I'm twenty-two. Claire is older than me. How can her stepfather refuse to let me see her? She's a grown woman for godssake."

"This is Ireland, Matt. They follow the old ways. Did you know that the first son is the sole inheritor of the farm?'

"So?"

"That means if there are other brothers, they're screwed. They get nothing."

"You mean the eldest son gets it all?"

"Yep."

"What do the other brothers do?"

"They move away. That's why a lot of them come to America. There's nothing for them here."

Matt shook his head in amazement. "What a system."

"As I said, they follow the old ways. As long as Claire is living under her father's roof, he calls the shots. That's just the way it is."

~~

Following one of Kerrigan's stockmen, an irritated Father Dunne gingerly picked his way through mud puddles and heaps of cow manure strewn on the path that led to the barn that housed Kerrigan's stable of horses. It was at times like this when he was certain that Kerrigan had absolutely no respect for a man of the cloth. The squire should have come up to the house to receive him instead of forcing an elderly man of the cloth to defile his shoes in this manner.

Kerrigan was feeding a carrot to a horse when Dunne came through the barn doors, stamping his feet to shake loose the cow manure he'd inadvertently stepped in.

Still feeding the horse, Kerrigan said, "You wanted to see me. What is it?"

"I've just had a chat with your man McCartan."

That got Kerrigan's attention. He spun around. "He's here in Ballyturan?"

"Aye, that he is. And him with a stiff attitude as well, I'll tell you that."

"What did he want?"

"It was the business of the letter all over again. Did I get the letter? Did I know his father?"

"And what did you tell him?"

"I told him I couldn't remember getting the letter and I did not know his father. Period."

"Did that satisfy him?"

"It did not. He as much as told me to my face that I was a liar. He'll burn in Hell for that he will."

Kerrigan pulled another carrot out of his pocket and turned his attention back to the horse. "Let me know if you hear anything else," he said, dismissively.

Father Dunne turned and winced as he realized he'd have to traipse back through that trail of shite.

As soon as the priest was gone, Kerrigan called out to a stockman in the back of the barn. "Terry, go into the village and tell Brian Heaney I want to see him straight away."

~~

Less than an hour later, Heaney came into the barn where Kerrigan was supervising the shoeing of his prize show horse. "Wait outside," he said to his farrier.

"Yes, sir," the man said, tipping his cap and scurrying out of the barn.

"Do you know young McCartan is in Ballyturan?" he asked the butcher.

"Aye. Didn't just this morning I see him looking into my shop window? He gave me a fright, I don't mind saying. He looks exactly like his father, he does. For a minute, I though Barry McCartan had come back from the dead."

"Has he spoken to you?"

Heaney eyes widened. "No. Why would he want to speak to the likes of me?"

"He's looking for information about his father. He's already spoken to Dunne. I expect he'll talk to anyone who will talk to him."

"Well, I'll have nothing to say to him. And that's a fact."

Kerrigan studied the butcher, trying to make up his mind whether to trust the ignorant man with the assignment he had in mind. Realizing he had no choice, he said, "Heaney, I want you to keep an eye on McCartan. Find out where he's staying, who he's speaking to. That sort of thing."

Heaney puffed up with pride that the squire should place such trust in him. "I will, Commandant. I'll report every move that he makes. You can count on me."

"Good man. Now off with you. And they'll be none of that commandant stuff."

"Aye, sir."

As the butcher hurried toward the door, anxious to get on with his mission, Kerrigan had a thought. "Heaney," he called after him, "do you still have that old pistol?"

Heaney's mouth went dry. "I do," he mumbled hoarsely. "And why would you be asking me that?"

"Nothing." Kerrigan waved a hand in dismissal. "All right, on your way."

~~

The next morning, Claire was walking on the road to the village when she saw Paddy coming toward her on his bicycle. When the hapless man spotted her, he attempted to impress her by executing a fancy skidding stop, but he only succeeded in skidding through a mud puddle and running himself—and his bicycle—off the road. Like most young men in the village, he was smitten by Claire and could always be counted on to do something clumsy or foolish in her presence. Doing his best to recover some degree of dignity, he pulled his bicycle out of the ditch, straightened his cap, and said, "Ah, well, Claire Twomey, did you meet the Yank then?"

"What Yank?"

"Sure the one I directed to your farm just yesterday."

"Yank? I met no…" Claire's stomach clenched. "Was his name Matthew McCartan by any chance?"

"I have no idea. He was a young, handsome chap. That's all I can say. He didn't give me his name."

"What did he say to you?"

"He wanted to know where the Twomey farm was. That's all."

"Oh… right… Good day to you, Paddy," she said absentmindedly and hurried on her way.

"And good day to you as well," a puzzled Paddy answered, tipping his cap.

As Claire neared the village, her head was spinning with questions. Could it be him, Matt McCartan? Had her half-brother come to Ballyturan? And if that was him, why hadn't he come to the farmhouse? And where would he be staying?

As she asked herself that last question, she had just come into the village and her eyes lit on the sign for the Kerrigan Arms.

~~

It had rained all night and a spectacular display of lightening and window-rattling thunder had kept Matt awake most of the night. Now it was just after eight and he stood by the window in his room gazing out at Dingle Bay. The storm had blown out to sea and an early morning fog drifted across the flat-calm sea.

About three hundred yards off shore, through the fog, he spotted a black object floating in the water. At first he thought it might be a whale, but as the fog lifted momentarily, he saw that it was some kind of odd looking boat. A lone fisherman, standing in the bow, cast his net into the sea. Then the fog settled back and he lost sight of the boat.

"Milk," a voice cried out. "'Tis fresh milk I have today."

1Matt looked down and saw an old man slowly leading a donkey cart containing two large galvanized tin milk canisters down the middle of the road. He shook his head and smiled. Ireland was indeed a country very different from his own. Try doing that in the middle of Second Avenue. This was his second day here and he he was still trying to adjust to this beautiful, mystical, mysterious land.

The land might be stunning, but he couldn't say as much for the people—at least the two people he'd met so far. His attempt to talk to the old priest and John Twomey had been exasperating. Was this the reaction he could expect from everyone he spoke to? It was beginning to dawn on him that this quest he had undertaken might be much harder than he'd thought it would be.

He was trying to decide on a new plan of action when a soft knock at the door pulled him from his thoughts. He opened it, expecting to see Karina, but instead, standing there was a young, attractive woman who looked vaguely familiar.

"Yes, may I help you?" he asked.

An apprehensive Claire stared at her half-brother, unable to speak. It had taken all her courage to come up to his room. In fact, if it weren't for Karina's encouragement, she wouldn't have come. But now that she was here, she didn't know what to say. She couldn't take her eyes off this man—her half-brother—who shared the same father. One thing was for sure—he looked nothing like the man she imaged from his letter. But what was he supposed to look like? she asked herself. What could she hope to tell from one letter? She couldn't help noticing that his hair was the same shade as hers. And there was something familiar about his eyes. Were they like hers? She wasn't sure.

Finally, she found her voice. "I'm Claire Twomey, your half-sister," she said softly.

Matt grabbed the door, feeling suddenly lightheaded. After all this time, he finally got to meet her. And now that she was standing in front of him, he was suddenly at a loss for words.

"Do you think I might come in?" she asked with an anxious smile.

"Oh, yes... of course... Please." He pointed to the bed. "Have a seat." No! He redirected her to the only chair in the room. He sat on the bed and immediately jumped up as though it were a hot stove. "Can I get you something?" He glanced around the tiny room. "Oh, I'm sorry. I'm afraid, there's nothing I can offer you."

He tried to pace the tiny room, but there was no place to go and he kept bumping into the furniture.

"Why don't you just sit down on the bed," she said quietly.

"Right." He sat down and slapped his hands on his knees. "Well."

"Well, indeed."

Self-consciously they stared at each other in awkward silence.

Claire spoke first. "So. You decided to come to Ballyturan. What a surprise."

"Surprise? I wrote you I was coming."

Claire frowned. "I received no such letter."

"Last May, in response to your letter, I wrote asking if your mother would be willing to speak to me. When I didn't get a response from you, I wrote you another letter in July saying I was coming to Ballyturan."

Claire shook her head in puzzlement. "I don't understand. I answered your 'to whom it may concern' letter. That's the last I heard from you."

"Now, I don't get it. What happened to the two letters I wrote you?"

Claire's eyes narrowed as she began to understand. "Was it you who came out to my farm yesterday?"

"Yeah. I met your father down by the road. I asked if I could see you, but he said no."

Now everything fell into place. "Old John—that's my stepfather—I think he has somehow intercepted your letters."

"But why would he do that?"

"I'm sure I don't know. I do know he's never wanted even a mention of your father's name. But what would he have against you, I have no idea."

"Have you told your mother about me?"

Claire shook her head. "No, I haven't. I don't think she'd want to be reminded of that bad business so long ago."

Matt nodded. He understood her position, but he was disappointed. It was vital that he speak to Claire's mother. After all, who would be able to answer questions about his father better than the girl he'd impregnated and abandoned? He stood up and went to the window to give himself a moment to think. From the expression on Claire's face, it was clear that this was very painful for her as well. Idly, as he watched the milkman below pouring milk into an old woman's pail, doubts began to creep into his mind. What the hell was he doing here in Ireland anyway? All he'd wanted was to find out who my father was, but all he was doing was dredging up painful memories for Claire and her mother. Was he being unnecessarily selfish? In the end, what did it really matter who his father was? And besides, maybe the answers he sought weren't here anyway. Maybe there were no answers to be found anywhere.

He turned away from the window. "Did your mother ever talk about my father? Did she say why he abandoned her?"

"Once, when I was little, my mum told me that old John wasn't my real father. She said my real father's name was Barry McCartan. She said when I got older, she'd tell me the whole story. Well, old John overheard her and there was a fearful row. He made her swear that she would never speak about him to me or anyone else again. And she never did."

Matt could see Claire's mother, the only direct link to his father, slipping away. In spite of his misgivings, he blurted out, "Would you ask her if she'd talk to me?"

With a stricken expression Claire stood up and smoothed her skirt. "Let me... let me think about it."

At the door, she impulsively gave him a hug. "I'm glad I met you, Matt McCartan," she said with tears in her eyes. "At least I think I am. I don't know." She shook her head. "It's all very confusing."

"Yeah, I know what you mean. It is confusing."

Matt walked her downstairs. Karina stood behind the counter with a big smile on her face. "So, a successful meeting of the McCartan clan."

"Sort of," Matt said with a shrug.

Claire hugged Karina. "Thanks. And remember, I was never here."

"I never saw you before in my life," Karina said with mock seriousness.

~~

The largest room in the small Twomey farmhouse was the kitchen, dominated by a fireplace that was used for both cooking and warmth. The furnishings were simple—a wooden table, flanked by two wooden benches, two additional wooden chairs next to the fireplace, and a cupboard that held the plates and utensils. The rest of the house consisted of two small bedrooms. The simple farmhouse was austere, but thanks to Maeve's careful attention to detail—pressed linen curtains on the two windows—it afforded a reasonably cozy environment for its three occupants.

At supper that night, Claire nervously watched old John for any sign that he knew she had seen her half-brother earlier. But, thankfully and, as usual, he had little to say except for the occasional grunt as he shoveled mutton stew into his mouth.

Much to her relief, right after supper, as was his habit, he went straight to bed. After Claire helped her mother clean the dishes, she sat down by the fire and pretended to read the newspaper while her mother busied herself mending her husband's sweater.

After awhile, old John's loud snoring told Claire that he was sound asleep. When he was in that state she knew not even the trumpet of Gabriel would wake him. Now she and her mother were alone. This was the moment she'd been waiting for—yet dreading. She put the newspaper aside and took a deep breath. After she'd left Matt's hotel room, she'd made up her mind that she would tell her mother about him. But now that the time had come, she was having second thoughts. How would her mother react to knowing that Barry McCartan's son was in Ballyturan? She studied her mother, deeply engrossed in her darning. The woman was only fifty-three, but she looked much older. Life with old John had not been easy on her. Still, Claire could see that her mother had once been very beautiful. And, in spite of her hard life, she still carried herself like a proud princess.

Claire cleared her throat. "Mum, there's something I want to show you."

Maeve looked up from her knitting. "Aye, what is it?"

Claire handed her mother Matt's letter. Maeve read it in silence. Then she turned her gaze to the fire and tears welled up in her eyes.

After a long, painful silence, Claire blurted out, "Mum, he's here in Ballyturan."

Her mother turned to her, bewildered. "Who is here?"

"Matthew McCartan. Barry McCartan's son," she said with emphasis, afraid that her mother might mistakenly believe Barry McCartan was here.

Maeve looked at the letter again. "Well, of course it couldn't be Barry. Doesn't it say here he's dead?"

Seeing the expression on her mother's face, Claire realized she'd made a terrible mistake. She'd never seen her look so unsettled or so desolate. There was no way she could ask her mother if she would want to meet Matt. Instead, she said, "I just thought you should know."

Maeve stood up and handed her daughter the letter. "I think I'll go to bed now."

As she disappeared into the bedroom, Claire dropped into a chair and stared morosely into the dying fire.

CHAPTER TWELVE

Matt woke to a steady drizzle beating against his window. He dressed and went down to the small dining room adjacent to the bar. He was surprised to see an elderly couple sitting in a corner. Until now, he had been the only guest in the hotel. He nodded to them and took a seat near the window where he could watch the rain beating down on the muddy road.

Karina came out of the kitchen with a pot of coffee. "How'd you sleep?"

"Better than the night before. Rain without the thunder is a lot better." He didn't tell her that loud cracks of thunder reminded him of incoming artillery and still scared the shit out of him.

She poured him coffee. "Well, if you like rain, you've come to the right place. The local joke here is that the only way you can tell the difference between winter and summer in Dingle is that the rain is warmer in the summer."

"Karina, I saw an odd looking black boat out on the bay the other morning. What is that?"

"That would be a currach. The design has been around since Neolithic times. They're made from wooden slats which are then covered in several layers of tar. And that particular currach belongs to Hugh Cleary. People around here say he's nuts, but I think he just likes to be alone. By the way, how did things go with Claire?"

"Inconclusive. I asked her to tell her mother I was here and she said she'd think about it."

"You have been a real shock to her system, Matt. She's conflicted. On one hand she wants to know everything about her mysterious half-brother, but she also realizes your presence will dredge up painful memories for her mother."

"I know," he said, needing no reminding that he was the proverbial unwelcome skunk at the garden party.

By the time Matt finished his breakfast of eggs, sausage and toast, the rain was no more than a heavy mist and he decided to walk down to the beach. Maybe the fresh salt air would help clear his troubled mind.

~~

A layer of fog blanketed the water, muffling the screeching of the gulls and terns. He started walking down the beach. About fifty yards away, he saw a man standing next to a black currach and realized it must be Hugh Cleary, the guy who was supposed to be nuts.

As Matt neared, he saw that fisherman was about to light his pipe. But then he looked up and gaped at Matt. The match burned his fingers and he had to drop it. Matt was beginning to get used to that reaction, but it still unnerved him.

"Good morning," Matt said.

"And good morning to you, sir."

Matt stuck out his hand. "Hi, I'm…"

"Sure don't I know who you are and you the mirror image of your da, Barry McCartan. Coming out of the fog like that, you gave me a start you did."

Matt felt a surge of excitement. "You knew my father?"

"Aye." He struck another match and this time succeeded in lighting his pipe. "Are you a Barry as well?"

"No. Matthew. And I believe you're Hugh Cleary?"

"Aye." He puffed on his pipe and silently stared out at the thick fog bank.

After an uncomfortable silence, Matt said, "When did you know my father?"

"Ah, since we were wee boys together," he said, still staring out at the fog shrouded sea.

Matt didn't know if Hugh was crazy, but he was certainly a man of few words.

"I've come here to find out about my father."

"And what is it that you didn't know?"

"Well, the truth is, my father didn't talk to me much, especially about anything personal. There's a great deal I don't know about him. Up until six months ago, I didn't even know he came from here."

"Well, as I remember, your da was a man of few words."

Matt, too, stared out at the fog, trying mightily to tamp down the frustration rising in him. He'd finally met someone who was willing to talk to him, someone who knew his dad, but it was like pulling teeth to get anything out of him. To his immense astonishment, almost like magic, the fog suddenly lifted, revealing a glassy sea. "Does fog always disappear so quickly?"

"Aye. And returns just as quickly. Have you ever been in a currach?" Hugh asked suddenly.

"No."

"Well, come on then. Give a hand."

Before Matt could protest that he wasn't fond of the water—actually he was terrified of the water ever since the day he'd almost drown at Coney Island when he was eight—he found himself helping Hugh.

Together, the two men slid the currach along the sand and jumped on board as the boat began to float. Hugh, nodding for Matt to sit in the stern, took hold of two massive wooden oars and with slow rhythmic strokes drove the boat away from the beach.

A nervous Matt glanced over his shoulder. "Um, how far out are we going?" he asked, clutching the sides of the boat.

"Just out a wee bit," Hugh answered, still puffing on his pipe.

With growing alarm, Matt noticed that the shoreline was quickly receding in the distance. It suddenly occurred to him that maybe this guy was crazy. "Do you think we should turn—" He stopped talking when he saw a solid wall of fog moving toward them. "Jesus Christ...!"

Hugh looked over his shoulder. "Ah, the fog is back."

Almost instantaneously, they were enveloped in a thick fog bank. Matt looked back toward shore, but he could see nothing. "Jesus Christ..." he muttered again.

Hugh put the oars down. "Well, there's nothing to be done but wait for it to lift."

"How long will that take?" Matt asked, fighting back panic.

"I don't know. Minutes. Hours."

"Hours... Why did you take me out here?"

"I only feel comfortable when I'm on the sea. The sea calms a man."

In spite of his anxiety, Matt had to admit that the motion of the the the currach, rising and falling on the gentle swells, was surprisingly soothing. And the eerie silence around them created an intimate feel, as thought Hugh Cleary and he were the only two people in the whole world.

"It was the ambush that drove you da from Ballyturan," Hugh said suddenly.

Matt stared at the fisherman. "Ambush?"

"Did you never hear about the Easter Uprising of sixteen?"

"It sounds vaguely familiar. Something about Irish rebels taking over the Post Office in Dublin."

"That would be Easter Monday, April the twenty-fourth. Me, your da, and most of the men in Ballyturan took part in that uprising. We were all in the Post Office that week until the British shelled up into submission."

"What happened to all of you?"

"The leaders—Pearse, and fourteen others, were executed by firing squad. The rest of us were thrown into prison. They released us the following June. And that's when the rumors started."

"What rumors?"

"That your da was an informer."

Matt felt his heart sink. Was that why he ran away? "Was he?"

"Ach, not a'tall. 'Twas only a vicious rumor. But there were some who believed it, I'll tell you that."

"What did my father do about it?"

"He tried to find out who it was that was spreading the rumor, but he never did discover who it was. It was around that time that Maeve told him she was pregnant."

"And that's when he ran away."

"No, he did not. Your da was an honorable man. The very next day he went into Dingle to find a priest who would marry them."

"Why wouldn't he get married here in Ballyturan?"

"Sure it would have been a scandal in this little village and didn't he want to avoid that?"

"You mentioned something about an ambush…"

Hugh knocked his pipe on the side of the boat and the ashes spilled out and drifted on the calm water. He took out a bag of tobacco and loaded the pipe and relit it. Matt watched the agonizingly slow ritual with growing impatience.

When Hugh was sure the pipe was well lit, he continued. "Jimmy Beggs and me were your da's best friends. We'd heard that a death sentence had been passed on him. We tried to talk him out of going to Dingle. We wanted him to run away, don't you know. But he wouldn't listen. He was stubborn that way. So Jimmy Beggs and me decided we would go with him to Dingle, like bodyguards you might say. We went all three armed with pistols."

There was a splash nearby and Matt jumped. "What was that?"

"Just a fish. Pay it no mind."

"It sounded like a big fish," Matt said, staring wide-eyed into the water.

"Probably just a shark."

"Probably just a…" Matt pointed toward shore. "Could we go back now?" Old Hugh Cleary was crazy and he didn't want to spend another minute on the boat with him.

"Do you know you're pointing out to sea?"

"What? How…?"

"Sure the boat has turned around. Didn't you feel it?"

"No, I didn't feel it," Matt said indignantly. "This is my first time on a currach." And my last, he said to himself.

"'Tis too dangerous to try to beach in this fog. The coastline here is wicked with rocks that would tear the bottom out of me boat."

Matt wanted to say he should have thought of that before they came out here. Instead, to take his mind off where he was and his precarious position, he decided it was best to just keep asking questions. "So the three of you went to Dingle?"

"Aye. He couldn't find a priest who would marry them, so we started for home early that evening. We were on the West Road just outside of Ballyturan when we were ambushed by four men. There was a fearful battle with guns blazing. When it was all over, three of the ambushers were shot dead. Your da had been shot in the leg. Jimmy Beggs took off into the woods after one that was trying to get away. We heard gunfire. While your da waited by the side of the road, I went looking for Jimmy. I found him dead. We never did find that fourth man."

Matt's mind was reeling from what Hugh had just said. "Your da had been shot in the leg..." Matt recalled his father always walked with a slight limp and he never knew why. Once he saw his father in his underwear and noticed a large scar on his left thigh. When Matt had asked what it was, his father dismissed it by muttering that he'd fallen on a pitchfork years ago. "Who were those men who tried to kill my father?"

"Later, we heard they was from Dublin. Members of an assassin group inside the Volunteers."

Matt could hardly believe what he was hearing. His father was a convicted informer? Hit men were sent out from Dublin to kill him? It was like something out of a very bad Hollywood melodrama. "Four men died. Was there an investigation?"

"Aye. But nothing came of it. As far as the constables were concerned, it was nothing more than a bunch of disorderly Volunteers killing each other and good riddance to them all."

"What happened to my father?"

"This time, he knew he had to run. If they sent out four men to kill him, they would send out more. He went up into the mountains. He took the bullet out of his own thigh, he did. I brought him food and clothing while he was recovering from his wound."

"Were you arrested?"

"And why would I be? Other than your da, and the Dublin man that got away, there were no witnesses. I never told a soul I was there that night."

Suddenly, the fog lifted. "I suppose you'll be wanting to go back?" Hugh asked.

"Yes, I would."

Hugh picked up the oars swung the boat in the direction of the shore and began to row. A relieved Matt jumped into the surf and helped Hugh drag the currach up onto the beach above the high water mark. Now that they were safely back on firm ground, Matt felt a whole lot better. Wanting to continue the conversation and hear more of his father's life he said, "So, how long did my father stay in the mountains?"

The fisherman shook his head and reached for his pipe. "Didn't I tell you I only feel comfortable when I'm on the sea? If you want to hear more of your da's story, you'll have to come out on the currach with me."

Matt studied the sea. It was calm now. Not at all threatening. But that's the way it looked before the fog dropped down on them. "Maybe later," he said. "But thanks for telling me about my father."

Hugh nodded, and without another word, turned and trudged up the hill toward his tiny shack.

A half a mile up the beach, crouched behind a sand dune, Heaney watched until Matt started back toward him and quickly slipped away.

~~

Ten minutes later, Heaney was in Kerrigan's study.

"Well, what do you have for me?" the Squire asked.

"The Yank found Hugh Cleary."

"Did they speak?"

"Aye."

"What did they talk about?"

"I dunno. I was too far away. Cleary took the Yank out on his currach and they disappeared into a fog bank. The man's daft, I tell ya."

"How long were they together?"

"A good half hour. Maybe more."

That was not welcome news to Kerrigan. Like everyone else in Ballyturan, he assumed that the unapproachable Cleary was, if not mad, at least peculiar in the head. As far as he knew, Cleary hadn't spoken to anyone in the village for years. So why did he talk to the young McCartan and what did he tell him?

With his head bowed, Heaney kneaded his cap in his hands and stared at the Persian rug beneath his booted feet. "I should have killed him back then," he muttered. "Besides Barry McCartan, Cleary was the only witness to what happened on the West Road that night. He could have informed on me, he could."

"Obviously, he didn't," Kerrigan said, weary of hearing the same lament from Heaney all these years.

"Why did you order me to do nothing, Commandant?"

"Because what happened that night was bad business. The Dublin men blundered and made a complete hash of it. Didn't we have the constabulary crawling all over the countryside for a fortnight? The last thing we needed was another murder for them to investigate." What Kerrigan didn't tell Heaney was that in spite of the botched assassination attempt, he got what he wanted. Namely, that Barry McCartan had had to run away. That was all that he really wanted. With McCartan out of the way, the business of the water was settled once and for all. Until now. What, he wondered yet again, did this young McCartan want?

"All right, Heaney. You're dismissed. Continue watching the Yank and report back to me what you observe."

Heaney jumped up. "Yes, Commandant. I'll do that."

~~

"I could use a drink," Matt said as he came through the door.

Karina closed a book she was reading. "You certainly look like you could use a drink. Come on, the bar's open."

By the time he'd finished his second Bushmills, he'd told Karina everything that Hugh had told him.

Karina shook her head. "Wow. It does sound like a bad Hollywood movie. So what's next?"

"I don't know. He won't talk to me unless I go back out on that damn currach."

"So?"

"So, I'm scared shitless of water. I almost drown when I was a kid."

"I feel for you. I've been claustrophobic ever since my big brother locked me in a closet when I was four."

Matt stood up. "I'm beat. I think I'll take a nap."

"Good idea. Sleep clears the mind."

CHAPTER THIRTEEN

Claire was feeding the chickens when her mother came out of the house, wiping her hands on her apron. "Would you like a cup of tea?" she asked.

"Aye, I would." Claire thought the question odd because it was only noon and they never had tea until four in the afternoon. Since she'd given her mother the letter from Matt, she seemed distracted and distant.

Inside, Maeve poured the tea. "I've been thinking about that letter."

Claire nodded, but said nothing, carefully watching her mother, trying to judge where this conversation was heading.

"I've decided I will meet this young man."

"Are you sure, Mum?"

"I've been thinking of nothing else since I read that letter. I'm sure."

"I'm so sorry for dredging up the past."

"Well, it wasn't you who did that. It was young McCartan who wrote the first letter."

"Aye, that's true. But I could have ignored it."

"Well, you didn't and that's that."

"When do you want to meet him?"

"I don't know. It can't be here. Your father must never know anything about this."

"I understand. He's staying at the hotel in the village. You could meet him there and—"

"No. Ballyturan is too full of chatterers."

"How about the beach?"

"Aye, I suppose that would be satisfactory. You make the arrangements, Claire."

~~

The next day, Karina was seated behind the counter, deeply engrossed in a textbook, when the door opened. She looked up and smiled. "Claire, what a pleasant surprise. What brings you to the big city?"

"My mum wants to meet Matt," Claire whispered, even though they were the only two in the room.

"Oh, boy. Is that good or bad?"

"I'm not sure. Have you seen Matt?"

"He's in his room. He met Hugh Cleary yesterday and what he heard about his father kind of rattled him."

"Why?"

"Something about your father being labeled an informer. Apparently, some guys tried to kill him."

"Oh, my God."

"Did you know anything about that?"

"No. The only thing I know about my father is his name. When I was just a baby, old John made my mother promise never tell me anything about him."

"So, it looks like Matt knows a hell of a lot more about your father than you do."

Claire bit her lip. "I don't know why, Karina, but I'm as jittery as a cat. I'm not sure I want to know anything about my father. And I'm not at all sure I want my mother and Matt to meet. Will it be a good thing or a bad thing? I just don't know."

"Well, the only way to find out is to... find out."

"I guess you're right."

~~

At the gentle knock at the door, Matt jumped out of bed. He'd been lying there for a good part of the afternoon, still trying to digest everything Hugh Cleary had told him. He opened the door and was surprised to see his sister standing there. "Claire. Come in, come in."

When she was seated, he said, "What brings you here?"

"My mother has agreed to meet you."

Matt slowly sat down on the bed. "Wow. Are you sure? I mean is she sure?"

"That's what she said."

"Well, that's great. When? Where?"

"Tomorrow on the beach. Eight o'clock."

~~

Matt was too nervous to eat the huge breakfast that Karina brought to him. "Wish me luck," he said, downing the remainder of his coffee."

"Luck," she called out after him as he rushed out the door.

A light misty rain began to fall just as he got to the beach. He checked his watch: Seven forty-five. As he paced up and down, his anxiety grew and troubling questions churned in his anxious mind. Was he doing the right thing? What was he doing in Ballyturan in the first place? Was it unfair to ask Claire's mother to dredge up what had to be a painful memory for her? Should he just...

"Matt McCartan?"

Startled at the sound of an unexpected voice, Matt spun around to face a woman wrapped in a black shawl. There was no doubting this was Claire's mother. They looked so much alike. He judged her to be in her fifties, but she was still an attractive woman and no doubt a very pretty girl in her youth. And this is the woman his father almost married. Now that she was standing there, he realized he didn't know how he should address her. Should he call her Maeve? Mrs. Twomey? Tentatively, he stuck his hand out. "Mrs. Twomey, I'm Matt McCartan."

Without warning, Maeve slapped his face. Hard.

He staggered back. "What—"

"How dare you."

"How dare I what...?"

Through tears, she shouted, "How dare you come here and dredge all this up again. I've spent my whole life trying to forget Barry McCartan and what he did to me and my daughter. It's taken me years to come to terms about what happened back then. And now you think you can just show up and turn everybody's lives upside down to satisfy some selfish whim to learn about your father."

"I'm sorry, Mrs. Twomey. I never intended to hurt you."

"Well, you have and you're a damn fool."

As she turned to leave, Matt called out. "Wait. Please. I want you to know that I knew nothing about what happened between you and my father. And I didn't know I had a half-sister. I only found out recently that my father came from here. I didn't come here to hurt you or anyone else. I came here..." Tears of frustration welled up in his eyes. "Why did I come here? I guess I came here to find out who the hell I am. You may find it hard to believe, but my father never talked to me. He never mentioned Ireland or you. I know nothing about my past or his. I'm just trying to find out who I am."

Maeve came toward him and gently touched his reddened face. "I'm sorry..."

"No, I'm the one who's sorry."

"For all these years, I've wanted to do that to your father. I had no right taking out my anger at him on you. You look so like your father," she said softly.

"Yeah, that's what everyone tells me."

"He was about your age when he... When he went away."

"You don't have to talk about it, Mrs. Twomey."

"Please, call me Maeve. Shall we walk?"

Matt was grateful to have something to do besides gaze into the eyes of this sad woman. Suddenly, a squall whipped in from the ocean. Lashed by the wind, the rain stung their eyes. But then, as quickly as it had come, it was gone. "You sure have very strange weather here," he said.

"That's the Dingle for you." She looked at him sideways. "But I'm sure you didn't travel all the way across that great ocean to talk to me about the weather."

"No, I didn't." He had so many questions to ask about his father, but now that he was face to face with her he didn't know where to begin.

"You'd like to know about your father."

"Yes. Yes, I would."

After a moment, she said, "Where to start? We grew up together. We went to school together. I think I was always in love with Barry... I mean your da. We talked about getting married, but that was not possible because he worked for his da and the financial prospects of a man working as a farmhand were not encouraging when it came to supporting a family. Then his father died and Barry inherited the farm. And that meant we could get married. But then the uprising came and changed everything. I begged him not to do it, but he joined the Volunteers in spite of my objections. He said all the lads were joining and he couldn't be the only one not to." She stopped to look out at the sea, and from her her expression she seemed to be reliving the events of so long ago in her mind's eye. "I've always wondered what life would have been like for us if he hadn't joined." She shrugged. "In any event, one morning he went off to Dublin with the other lads."

"I heard it turned out badly."

"Aye. He was lucky he wasn't shot or hanged. I was grateful for that. But they did keep him in prison until June of seventeen. When he came back, he looked terribly haggard and had lost a good deal of weight. But I was so happy. Thank God, he'd given up any notion of fighting the British. We began to make plans to marry. Then one day he came to me, looking very serious and told me that there was a rumor going around that he was an informer. Of course it was preposterous. He went to Squire Kerrigan who was the commandant of the Volunteers at that time. Kerrigan assured him that there was nothing to the rumor and he should just put it out of his mind. But Barry didn't trust Kerrigan. There was bad blood between them because of the water rights. Still, the rumors seemed to die down for a time. Then, I..."

Maeve abruptly stopped and turned away to face the sea, but not before Matt saw that her pale cheeks had turned a deep shade of crimson. "God have mercy on me..." she said in a soft whisper, "I... I got pregnant." She took a deep breath and continued walking. "I'll never forget the day I told your da. I was riding into the village with him on his cart. It was market day, usually an exciting time with folks coming from villages near and far to sell their livestock and wares. It was a chance to meet old friends and for the men to share a pint and the women to catch up on the latest gossip. But on that day my entire world turned upside down."

"How did he react when you told him?" In spite of what Hugh had said, he still harbored the suspicion that it was news of the pregnancy that had made him run away.

"He was so happy—and I was so relieved. He said he would go to Dingle the very next day to find a priest who would marry us straight way. We both knew Father Dunne would have nothing to do with us."

"So what went wrong?"

"While we were in the market, Barry met a fellow Volunteer from a neighboring village who'd been in prison with him. He told Barry that it was not a rumor. He had been found guilty by a secret court of being an informer and his life was in danger."

"What did he do?"

"Your father had a stubborn streak. He refused to be cowed. He said he would wait for someone to accuse him to his face and then he would deal with it."

Matt was baffled. He tried to square the man she was describing with the father he knew. It seemed like they were two different people. One defiant, the other apathetic.

Maeve pulled the shawl around her to protect her from a sudden gust of wind. "The next morning, I went to his farm to see him off. Jimmy Beggs and Hugh Cleary were there as well. They were having a great row about his decision to go to Dingle. They wanted him to go into hiding. But he wouldn't hear of it. As a compromise, he agreed that they would go to Dingle with him. I watched the three of them head off down the road..." Tears welled up in her eyes. "And that's the last time I laid eyes on your da."

"Did you know they were armed?"

Maeve looked at him wide-eyed. "No, I did not."

"Hugh Cleary filled me in. On the way back from Dingle they were ambushed by four men—apparently sent to carry out the court's sentence."

"Oh, my God..."

"When it was over three assassins were dead. One got away. My father was shot in the leg and Jimmy Beggs was killed."

"I never knew the whole story of what happened that night. The next day, constables and men in civilian clothes swarmed into Ballyturan. They questioned a lot of people, but they never told us what had happened. And everyone was too afraid to ask. We knew that Jimmy Beggs was dead, but we heard nothing about those four men. For days I cried day and night, sure that Barry had been shot dead. A week later, I was on my way to mass when Hugh came riding up on a bicycle. He didn't stop. As he rode by, he looked straight ahead, but out of the side of his mouth he muttered, 'Barry is alive.' And then he was gone. I sat down in the middle of the road and cried for an hour."

"Why didn't he stop to talk to you?"

"It was a frightening time then with constables and policemen in civilian clothes roaming the countryside. There were rumors that some in the village had turned informer and that there were spies everywhere. Neighbor distrusted neighbor. It took years for things to get back to normal."

Maeve turned around and looked up the beach. "I should be getting back."

"Of course. Maeve, I can't thank you enough. I know this has been very hard for you."

"Aye, it has. But at the same time, much to my surprise, it's been liberating as well. Till this moment, I've not told a soul what I've told you. The remembering has been painful, but it's also been good to finally be able to talk about it to someone."

"If I need to talk to you again, how can I get in touch with you?"

"You must never come to the farm." She thought a moment. "Do you know Karina at the hotel?"

"Yes."

"Use her as a contact. She and Claire are thick as thieves."

"Okay. I'll do that."

As they walked back up the beach, each lost in thought about what had been said, they failed to notice Heaney crouched behind a sand dune.

~~

"My own wife consorting with the likes of him," Twomey shouted indignantly. "Jaysus, Mary and Saint Joseph, what a state of affairs this is."

"Now, now," Father Dunne hissed. "There'll be no taking the Lord's name in vain in my presence."

"Stop it, the two of you. There's no time for petty squabbling," chided Squire Kerrigan, who had summoned Dunne and Twomey to his home to hear Heaney's report. "According to Heaney, young McCartan has met with Hugh Cleary and now Maeve. The question is, what does that mean?"

"The answer to that question," Father Dunne said, "depends on what each of them knows."

Heaney jabbed his thick finger in the air. "I can tell you what Cleary knows. He knows I was there that night."

"Nonsense," Kerrigan countered. "If he had recognized you, he would have given you up to the constables."

"Not necessarily," Dunne said. "Hugh Cleary had as little use for the authorities as the rest of us."

"And that's a fact," Heaney said, nodding vigorously. "So just because he didn't inform on me, doesn't mean he didn't see me."

Kerrigan slammed his hand on his desk. "It's a moot point, Heaney. If he's told no one after all these years, it doesn't really matter. What does Maeve know?" he asked Twomey.

The old farmer shrugged. "I dunno. Of course she knew a great deal about Barry McCartan up until the night of the shooting. But I don't think she had any contact with him after that." He slammed his fist on his knee. "But, I tell you, I will question her and get to the bottom of it."

"You'll do no such thing," Kerrigan said.

"And why not?"

"It's best that Maeve and Claire and young McCartan don't know that we're on to them. That way Heaney can keep an eye on McCartan and you can keep an eye on your wife and daughter. Is that understood?"

Twomey scowled, but he nodded in the affirmative.

Kerrigan stood up, signaling the meeting was over. "Heaney, you will continue to watch McCartan. Twomey, you know what you have to do. Dunne, you will inform me of any information you receive."

"I will not violate the sacred confessional oath of clergy-penitent privilege."

"No one's asking you to do that, man. There's plenty you hear outside the confession box. Just keep your ears open."

~~

The elderly couple, still the only other guests in the hotel, had just finished their breakfast and were heading out of the dining room.

"Good luck with your search," Karina called after them. They waved and then were gone.

"Nice old couple," Karina said, pouring Matt another cup of coffee. "From Dayton, Ohio. They're here to seek the birthplace of the man's father. Personally, I think they're barking up the wrong peninsula. They mentioned a couple of towns, but they're all on the east coast."

"It's not easy for us ancestral seekers."

"Speaking of which, did you know your father owned a farm?"

"Yeah. Maeve mentioned it. How did you know?"

"I was visiting one of my Irish speakers yesterday and I happened to mention that you were here looking for information on you father. He's an old-timer and he remembered your father. He said your dad owned a farm out on the Falls Road next to Squire Kerrigan's spread. He said it was small but, as he recalled, it had been in the McCartan family for generations."

Matt stirred his coffee. "Isn't that weird? My father never mentioned anything about a farm in Ireland. Of course," he added with a note of irony, "he never mentioned much of anything."

"Do you realize you own that farm?"

The question startled him. "No. Surely it must have been sold years ago."

"Who could have sold it? Your father was the sole owner of the land. I'm no expert on Irish real estate law but, as his only heir I would think the land belongs to you."

"What about Claire?

"Yeah, I guess her, too." Karina grinned. "You want to become a farmer?"

"Not hardly."

"Well, I think you should at least check it out."

"I don't even know where it is."

"I do. It's about two miles out on the Falls Road right next to Kerrigan's farm. Have you been out that way?"

"No."

"You can't miss it. Look for the big mansion on the hill that looks like a cross between Tara and the White House. That will be Squire Kerrigan's humble home. Your farm is just to the east of that."

Matt pushed his cup away. Coffee was beginning to give him heartburn. "I don't know. Sounds like a wild goose chase to me."

Karina poked his shoulder playfully. "Hey, what have you got to lose? You may be the inheritor of a grand estate."

"Right."

"I have an old rusty bike out back. You can take that. The ride and the fresh air will do you good."

~~

It had been awhile since Matt had ridden a bike and he was a little shaky, especially trying to negotiate the rut-scarred dirt roads. It was nothing like riding a bike on Second Avenue. But then again, here he didn't have to worry about dodging taxies and trucks. The Kerrigan mansion was just as Karina had described it. The enormous house was startlingly out of place among the modest farms that dotted the hillsides around it.

The entrance to the Kerrigan estate was marked by an impressively large wrought iron arch anchored by two stone pillars. A well-maintained gravel road wound its way up the hill toward the house. Karina had said his father's farm was just to the east from Kerrigan's, but he hadn't seen an entrance lane. He backtracked on foot and about a hundred yards down the road, he saw the faint outline of what must have been a lane at one time. Leaving the bike on the side of the road, he trudged up the hill.

At the top of a rise, he came to a small farmhouse, or at least what was left of it. The thatched roof had long since crumbled, revealing worn and weathered roof beam joists. The once whitewashed walls were grey from weather and lack of maintenance. There was something sad about this wreck of a house. And then he realized why. It was a metaphor for his father's life—initially purposeful, but now neglected and lifeless. This is where his father was born and raised. And, if that old Irish speaker was to be believed, it was also the home of his grandfather and his great-grandfather. Why had his father abandoned the farm? Was it the business of being labeled an informer? Was it fear or shame at the prospect of becoming a father? And why had he never mentioned the farm to his own son?

Shaking those troubling thoughts from his head, Matt continued up the lane. About fifty yards beyond the house, he came to a very large pond. He'd come here expecting to find an abandoned farm but, judging by the number of cows and sheep that were drinking and milling about, obviously the farm was owned by someone.

"You there," a voice shouted. "What are you doing here?"

Matt turned and saw two men glaring at him. The elderly white-haired one was dressed in a tweed jacket and, oddly enough, riding breeches and high boots. He'd seen men similarly attired in Central Park horseback riding. The other man, young and beefy, was cradling a shotgun.

The man in the tweed jacket, and obviously the one in charge, said, "I repeat, what are you doing here?"

"I think my father used to own this land. I just came to have a look."

"Squire Kerrigan, here, owns the land," the man with the shotgun said. "And you're trespassing."

Matt didn't like his tone. He took a step toward him and the man leveled the shotgun toward his chest. Suddenly, Matt heard a buzzing in his head and his senses became alive. Being in more hand-to-hand combats than he cared to remember, he began to size up his adversary. His opponent was big, but he looked slow. Matt mentally measured the distance between them. One more step, and he'd be in striking range. His old instincts kicked in and he knew what he would do next without even thinking about it. Lunge, kick toward the groin, grab the weapon, swing the butt and smash it into his face, stand over the prostrate body, point the weapon at his face, and—pull the trigger.

Kerrigan, perhaps seeing the murderous look in Matt's face, or just wanting to avoid further escalation, pushed the shotgun barrel up into the air. "Now, now. That's enough of that. Just leave now and there'll be no trouble."

As quickly as it came, the buzzing in Matt's head ceased and he felt the adrenaline drain from him. "My name is Matt McCartan. I meant no harm. I was told that this might be my father's farm and I just wanted to have a look."

"Well, you have. Now off with you."

Matt started to leave, but then he stopped and turned around. Fixing his gaze at the pond, he said, "Mr. Kerrigan, do you own this farm?"

"I do."

"Did you buy it from my father?"

"I don't care to discuss my business with strangers. Be on your way."

As Matt made his way down to the road, he recalled Maeve having said something about bad blood between his father and Kerrigan over water rights. What, he wondered, did that mean?

~~

He found Karina in the dining room folding napkins. "Well, I guess I'm not about to become landed gentry after all," he said.

"What a shame. I was hoping for an excuse to have a celebratory drink."

"Let's have one anyway."

"Good idea."

In the bar, she poured them both a whisky.

"So how is it that you're not going to be landed gentry?"

"Because the land belongs to your employer."

"The squire?"

"The same."

"Did your father sell him the farm?"

"Kerrigan didn't answer that question directly. But he led me to believe that he does own it."

"Wait a minute, Matt. There's something fishy going on here. Again, I'm no expert in Irish real estate law, but it seems to me that the only one who could sell that farm was your father. If he was on the run from those Dublin men, when would he have had time to sell it?"

Matt thought about that for a moment. "That's a good question and I don't have an answer."

"Who would?"

"I don't know. Maeve said the last time she saw my father was when he went off to Dingle that morning. So, she wouldn't know. That leaves Hugh Cleary. Maybe he knows something."

Karina looked into his face. "Why so glum?"
"Because it means another ride in that damn currach."
Karina tried, but failed, to suppress a smile. "You poor man."

Chapter Fourteen

The next morning, an anxious Matt was on the beach before dawn. He didn't know Hugh's schedule, so he decided he would be on the beach, hopefully before the old fisherman set out for his day's fishing. He saw the upturned currach on the beach. A good sign. He was about to go up to the old shack on the hill, when he saw Hugh coming down.

"Good morning," Matt said.

Hugh grunted, puffing on his pipe.

"I had a couple of questions," Matt said tentatively. "If you've got a moment—"

"Give a hand here," Hugh said, nodding at the currach.

"Sure. But I thought, before you head out, if I could just ask you—"

"On the boat, on the boat."

Acknowledging defeat, Matt helped to turn the boat over and together they pushed it into the surf. Dutifully, Matt took his seat in the stern and looked fearfully out to sea. Mercifully, the sea was calm and there was no sign of fog. At least not at the moment.

Hugh waited until they were several hundred yards off shore before he put the oars down. "Well, what are your questions?"

"I heard there was bad blood between my father and Kerrigan over water rights."

"True. 'Tis true. Kerrigan with his great big farm did not have water enough for his livestock, but your da's farm did. When your grandda died and your da took over, he told Kerrigan that the present arrangements over the water rights were not fair. That old skinflint Kerrigan didn't want to pay what was right and proper, but in the end your da got what he wanted. Your da could be a stubborn man," Hugh added with a slight smile playing around his lips.

"Before my father ran away, did he sell the farm to Kerrigan?"

"He did not. He would never sell that farm to the likes of Kerrigan."

"I spoke to Kerrigan yesterday. He led me to believe he owns the farm."

"He does not," Hugh said indignantly. "He's just using the land for his livestock."

"Is he allowed to do that?"

"Who's to stop him?"

"I don't know… The authorities…"

"And why would they care? Kerrigan has powerful influence around here. If there were no complaints, why should the authorities stir up the pot?"

Hugh took the pipe out of his mouth and stared at it pensively. "For years there, I kept hoping your da would come back to reclaim his farm. But…" He cleared his throat. "Yer man Kerrigan has been telling everyone he bought the land, but he's a damnable liar, he is."

"How do you know all this?"

Hugh banged the bowl of the pipe against his knee, dislodging the ashes. Then, he went through the same agonizingly slow ritual of loading it and lighting it. He took a satisfying puff. "How do I know, you ask?" Matt saw that same faint smile playing around his lips. "Because everyone in Ballyturan thinks I'm tetched."

"Why do they say that?"

"Because I don't talk to anyone. And because they think I'm tetched, they say things in my presence that they wouldn't say otherwise. Like I was a child, don't you know? I know more about what's going on in this village than anyone else dead or alive."

"Forgive me for asking, but you live alone here, almost like a hermit. Why is that?"

"I have my reasons," Hugh said, evasively. He turned around and reached for the large net in the bow. "Would you like to fish now?"

"What! No, no, thanks." Matt looked anxiously over his shoulder at the beach. It was less than a few hundred yards away, but to him it looked like twenty miles. "If you could just drop me off on the beach that would be great."

"Nothing like fishing to clear the mind and feed the soul." When he saw that Matt wasn't interested, he shrugged. "As you wish," he said, taking up the large oars.

~~

Over dinner that evening, Matt recounted to Karina what Hugh had told him.

"Maybe Hugh is wrong," she said. "Maybe, somehow, Kerrigan was able to buy the farm."

"I guess that's possible, but I'm not sure I want to take the word of a man whom everyone thinks is nuts."

"You're probably the only person in Ballyturan to have a meaningful conversation with him in God-knows-how-many years. Do you think he's wacky?"

Matt thought for a moment. "No, I don't think so. Eccentric? Definitely. Nuts? No."

Karina stood up to clear away the dishes. "Here's my two cents for what it's worth. Don't take his word for it. Find out for yourself."

"How?"

"Thomas O'Doherty."

"Who's that?"

"A solicitor in Dingle. I used him to help me when I was applying for a work visa. He's a nice old guy and very efficient."

"A solicitor? Is that like a lawyer?"

"Not exactly. In Ireland, the guy who argues cases in court is called a barrister. A solicitor is someone who handles the paperwork and such."

"And you think I should go see him?"

"Yeah. He'll be able to research the farm's title and see who really owns it."

"Okay. I'll go first thing in the morning."

"Take my bike. It's a long walk."

~~

After a shaky ride and more than a few delays while he waited for herds of cows and sheep to cross the road, Matt finally made it to Dingle. The town was not very large, but compared to Ballyturan, it looked like a bustling city. Following Karina's instructions, he made his way to Strand Street. About half way down the street he saw a sign posted over a painted green door that stated: Thomas R. O'Doherty, Solicitor.

The office was small and dark with the slightly musty, but not unpleasant, odor of old books and paper. Seated at a desk covered with folders and files was an elderly gentleman. He looked up and regarded Matt over his wireless glasses. "Good morning, sir. May I be of service?"

"Are you Mr. O'Doherty?"

"I am."

"My name is Matt McCartan. Karina Jaworski suggested I come see you."

"Karina...? The name doesn't ring a bell."

"She works at the Kerrigan Arms Hotel in Ballyturan. She came to you for some help securing a work visa."

"Ah, yes. The young lady who came here to study the Irish speakers. Now I remember. A lovely young woman. How is she getting on?"

"Fine."

"And how may I be of service to you, Mr. McCartan?"

"My father had a farm in Ballyturan, but he left many years ago. I'd like to know who presently owns the farm."

"Did he sell it?"

"I'm not sure."

"Are there heirs?"

"Just me." Then he thought of Claire. All his life he'd assumed he was his father's only child. But now that was no longer true. "I mean me and a half-sister," he corrected himself. "We had the same father."

"I see. Well, if he didn't sell it, then I should think you and your sister own the farm."

"A Mr. Kerrigan says he owns it."

"Would that be Squire Kerrigan?"

"Yes."

"Well, the squire owns a good deal of land on the Dingle Peninsula. I can tell you that. Do you think maybe your father sold the farm to him?"

"I don't know. That's why I'm here."

"Quite so. Quite so." He reached for a pen and began to write. "Matt McCartan. And where are you staying in Ballyturan?"

"The Kerrigan's Arms."

O'Doherty made a note and consulted his calendar. "This shouldn't take long." He stood up and offered his hand. "Come back in two days and I'll have an answer for you."

Matt shook O'Doherty's hand. "I'm surprised you can do it that quickly. In New York this kind of search would probably take weeks."

The old man smiled. "This is Ireland, Mr. McCartan. A small country. And Dingle is even a smaller piece of it. I'll see you on Thursday."

~~

Heaney found Kerrigan in a field, feeding an apple to his prize horse, Blathmac.

"Well, Heaney, what is it?"

"Yesterday morning, young McCartan went to see Hugh Cleary again. Then this morning, he rode on a bike on the road to Dingle."

Kerrigan spun around. "Dingle?" he asked sharply. "Why?"

"I don't know, Squire."

Kerrigan studied the butcher with distain. As a spy, the man was hopeless. But it was all he had. "Very well. Keep me posted."

"I will, sir." Heaney touched his cap and left.

Alone again, Kerrigan thought about his encounter with McCartan the day before. The young man not only looked like his father, he had that same pugnacious way about him. Barry McCartan had been a thorn in his side then, and now it looked like his son would be, too. Why, he wondered, had McCartan asked about the ownership of the farm? And it hadn't escaped his notice that the young man seemed to be very interested in the pond. He was brought out of his thoughts by the approach of one of his gardeners.

"Squire Kerrigan, Father Dunne is here to see you."

"Well, tell him to come down to the field."

"I did, sir, but he begs your pardon. He says he's turned his ankle and is having trouble walking."

"Very well."

~~

Kerrigan found Dunne in his study, flipping through the pages of a book.

"Ah, Squire," the priest said, returning the book to its place on the shelf, "it's a lovely library you have here. Just lovely."

"Yes, yes. What can I do for you?"

The priest suddenly turned very solemn. "May I sit down?"

Kerrigan motioned him into a chair and he sat down at his desk. "Well, what is it?"

Dunne rubbed his hands together. "I've been thinking about that young McCartan boy."

Kerrigan grunted. "It seems we all have."

"I've been thinking, maybe it would be best to just come clean with him."

"About what?" Kerrigan asked sharply.

"I mean like…. I should tell him about my part in… in what Maeve did."

"Why would you want to get into that?"

"My conscience has been troubling me since the first day I spoke to him. I told him a lie, and, God forgive me, I've been living with that lie ever since. I kept thinking that he would go away. But he hasn't. It's been over a week and he's still here. He'd bound to come across the truth eventually."

Kerrigan looked at the priest carefully. "What is the truth, Dunne? What exactly do you want to tell him?"

"Well, that… that I advised Maeve to marry Twomey and—"

"Advised or coerced?"

"I did no such thing," the priest said, indignantly.

"Really? Then why did you threaten her and her mother with the Magdalene laundries? And are you going to tell McCartan why Twomey paid for a new roof for you church?"

Dunne fell back in his chair. "How did you know…?" He voice trailed off and he fell silent. Of course he knew exactly how Kerrigan knew these things. Didn't he have spies and informers everywhere? Some he paid, but others did it simply to curry favor with him. There wasn't much that went on in Ballyturan that Squire Kerrigan didn't know about. "There's no need to tell him everything," the priest said quietly. "Just enough to satisfy his curiosity so he'll go back to America."

"That won't do, Dunne. Once you open Pandora's box, there'll be no stopping him. He'll want to know everything. Do you hear? Everything."

The priest hung his head in defeat. "Yes… I suppose you're right."

"Don't worry," Kerrigan said in a more solicitous tone. "I'm keeping an eye on McCartan. He'll learn only what we want him to learn."

After Dunne left, Kerrigan poured himself a brandy and went out to the terrace. In the field across the way, Blathmac was slowly trotting the perimeter, looking for a young filly to impress.

He sat down on a stone bench and thoughts of his conversation with the priest drifted into his mind. It was circumstances—or plain bad luck—that had locked him in this involuntary collusion with Dunne, Heaney, and Twomey. They had not consciously entered into a conspiracy against Barry McCartan, but by their actions each of them had done something to adversely affect his life in some way. It was like a jigsaw puzzle that he feared someone as tenacious as young McCartan might be able to solve. And the outcome would not be good for any of them. Since the arrival of that first letter, Kerrigan had been uneasy, wondering which one of them would be the first to break. Which one of them would confess to young McCartan the part they played in the life of Barry McCartan? Well, now he knew. Father Dunne was the weak link in the chain. And Heaney would have to add the priest to his watch list.

~~

Early Thursday morning, Matt rode Karina's bike into Dingle. True to his word, Mr. O'Doherty had completed his research. The old man rooted through piles of paper on his cluttered desk until he found what he was looking for. "Ah, here it is," he said waving a folder.

Now that the moment of truth had arrived, Matt was anxious. If it turned out that he and Claire owned the farm, what would they do with it? On the other hand, if they didn't own the farm, how did Kerrigan get it?

O'Doherty squinted at the report in front of him. "After exhaustive research into the matter, I could find no bill of sale or transfer of title to the farm."

"What does that mean?"

O'Doherty looked at Matt over his wire rimmed glasses. "It means, Mr. McCartan, that you and your sister are the sole owners of the property."

"But what about Kerrigan's claim?"

"Unless he can produce a bill of sale or transfer of title, he has no claim. Pure and simple."

"So it's possible that Kerrigan has been using my father's land all these years illegally?"

"It would seem so. And just between you and me, I wouldn't be at all surprised. Let's just say that Squire Kerrigan does not have a sterling reputation when it comes to his business affairs."

Matt could feel the anger rising in him. "That sonofabitch threatened me on my land. What chutzpah."

The old solicitor leaned forward with a puzzled expression. "Chutzpah?"

"It's an old Yiddish expression meaning… I guess you would say, cheeky."

He sat back. "Ah, that would describe the squire well."

"Well, what's next, Mr. O'Doherty?"

"Ask the squire to produce proof of ownership. If he can't,"— O'Doherty slipped the report across the desk toward Matt—"show him that. It's a notarized finding from Land Registry stating that the farm is owned by one Barry McCartan. And, absent a will to the contrary, you and your sister are the sole beneficiaries of your father's estate and are the rightful owners of the farm. There is some paperwork that must be filed with the court to bring everything up to date. Would you like me to proceed with that?"

"No, not yet, Mr. O'Doherty."

"As you wish," O'Doherty said, standing up. "If I can be of further assistance to you, please don't hesitate to let me know."

"I will. Thank you for all your help."

~~

Matt slapped the report from the Land Registry Office down on Karina's desk and grinned. "Well, it looks like Claire and I own a farm."

"That's great. Now what? Are you going to drive Squire Kerrigan's herds off your land?"

"Not yet."

"Why?"

"Believe me, I would like nothing more than to confront that arrogant sonofabitch and shove this report down his throat, but now isn't the time."

"Because?"

"Because there so much more I want to learn about my father. If I toss Kerrigan off the land now, he'll see to it that no one in Ballyturan ever speaks to me again."

"Yeah, you've got a point. He wields a lot of influence around here. Are you going to tell Claire?"

"No, not yet. For the time being, the fewer people who know about this, the better."

~~

Market day brought the usual assortment of farmers into Ballyturan to sell, barter, or trade everything from cows to pigs to potatoes and cabbage. It was late afternoon and most of the business of the marketplace had been concluded. By tradition, most of the farmers converged on Kerrigan's Pub to share a pint and, depending on which side of the transaction he was on, grumble about how he'd been swindled into paying far too much for a scrawny cow—or not getting a fair price for such a fine specimen.

Kerrigan, Twomey, and Heaney sat at a table in the rear of the pub, away from prying eyes.

"What have you to report?" Kerrigan asked.

The butcher took a swig of his porter and wiped the foam off his mouth with his sleeve. "Yesterday morning, he went back into Dingle, he did."

"And what was the purpose of his business?" Twomey asked.

"I'm sure I don't know. Am I a mind reader?"

Twomey thumped the table with his closed fist. "Squire, let me question Maeve and Claire. They must know something."

"No," Kerrigan said sharply. "They must not know we're on to McCartan."

"But we're not on to him." Twomey countered. "All we know is that he went into Dingle a couple of times. Why? What was he doing there? Do you have answers to those questions, Squire?"

"Not yet. But, by God, I will. Now off with the both of you."

Heaney and Twomey went away grumbling.

Kerrigan watched them go. Grudgingly, he had to admit the quarrelsome Twomey was right. They knew next to nothing about McCartan's intentions. He would have to do something about that.

~~

Kerrigan was driving his trap on the road just outside of the village when a man dressed in a dark blue suit stepped into the roadway. The squire recognized the sharp-featured, baldheaded man. Brian Mullen was a clerk in the government office in Dingle. In the past he'd been useful in obtaining proprietary information that had on more than one occasion helped him seal a deal to his great advantage.

Kerrigan reined in the horse. "Did you want to see me, Mullen?"

"I did, Squire. I believe I have some useful information for you."

"All right, get in."

Mullen climbed into the trap and Kerrigan snapped the reins. The horse immediately broke into a slow trot.

"Well, what is it?"

Even though they were on a deserted road with no one in sight, Mullen's eyes darted about like a ferret's, as though he expected to be overheard. "Do you know a solicitor named Thomas O'Doherty?" he said nervously.

"The name rings a bell, but I can't say I know him." That was a lie. A couple of years earlier, Kerrigan had hired O'Doherty to handle some legal transactions for him. He found the man to be infuriatingly honest, refusing to bend the rules even one jot. That was the first and last time he employed the services of Thomas O'Doherty. "Why do you ask?"

Mullen kept glancing around. "A couple of days ago, the solicitor came into the Land Registry Office requesting a land title search."

Kerrigan felt his stomach tighten. Forcing himself to remain calm, he said, "And what land was he looking at?"

"The McCartan farm."

Kerrigan knew the answer, but he asked the question anyway. "Do you know who O'Doherty was working for?"

"He was there on behalf of one Matthew McCartan."

"I see." Kerrigan stopped the trap and handed a pound note to Mullen. "Thank you for the information."

"It's always a pleasure." Mullen climbed down from the trap. "If I can be of further service...."

"Yes, yes," Kerrigan said dismissively. "I'll let you know."

He snapped the reins and the horse resumed trotting. Kerrigan detested others knowing his business, but in Mullin's case it couldn't be helped. Still, the clerk had no trouble accepting bribes and because of that, Kerrigan didn't trust him. He lived in dread that one day one of his enemies would bribe Mullen to tell all that he knew about Kerrigan's business dealings.

And now, at least three people—McCartan, O'Doherty, and Mullen— knew that he didn't own the farm. The thought of being humiliated and losing the respect of everyone on the Dingle Peninsula was abhorrent to him. From the first day he'd uttered the lie that he owed the farm, he dreaded that one day someone would appear and make him out to be a liar, a thief, and a fraud. He had spent seventy-eight years of his life building a reputation. He was Squire Kerrigan, the lord of all he surveyed. It was unthinkable that all that could be taken away from him by some young pugnacious Yank. Something had to be done with him.

As he neared his estate, he willed his panic into submission and he began to coolly assess the problem confronting him. What options did he have? Would McCartan consider a fair payment for the water rights? Kerrigan was a skilled negotiator, but recalling the obstinacy and pig-headedness of his father all those years ago, he doubted the son would agree to a fair and reasonable solution. He could offer to buy the farm. But would McCartan sell it to him at a fair price or use the leverage of the water rights to gouge an exorbitant price from him?

One thing was for certain. Whatever agreement they came to would have to be conducted in the strictest secrecy. No one must ever learn what he had done.

~~

Over dinner that night alone in the great hall, Squire Kerrigan continued to brood over his options. Now that he'd had time to think about it, he realized that those options of this afternoon were wildly unrealistic. There was no way that McCartan would accept a fair price for the water rights. And there was no way he would sell the farm for a fair price. No doubt, McCartan blamed him for his father's flight from Ballyturan and he would want his revenge. He would want to exact his pound of flesh no matter the consequences.

Bleakly, he realized he had only one option left. As a servant came in to clear the dishes, he said, "Mary, send someone into the village to fetch Heaney. I want to see him immediately."

Chapter Fifteen

It was after ten by the time Heaney was shown into Kerrigan's study. "Good evening, Commandant," he said, swiping his cap off his head. "You wanted to see me?"

Normally, Kerrigan would have told him to stop referring to him as "Commandant," but under the circumstances, perhaps it was best that Heaney think he was about to engage in a military operation.

Kerrigan pointed to a chair by the fireplace. "Sit down, Heaney. Would you like a drink?"

The butcher was taken aback—and not only because of the squire's cordial tone. In all the times he had been summoned to the the estate, not once had the man ever offered him a drink. "I... I think I would, Squire," he said, uncomfortably sitting on the edge of a plush side chair. "If... if it's not too inconvenient," he added quickly.

Kerrigan filled two glasses with brandy and gave one to Heaney.

"To your health, sir," Heaney said, raising his glass.

Kerrigan nodded and sat down on a matching chair opposite Heaney. "Do you still have that pistol?" he asked abruptly.

The question stunned Heaney. This was the second time the squire had asked that question. "Yes, yes, I do," he answered, wondering where this conversation was leading.

"Heaney, remember awhile back you told me how bad you felt about failing in your mission to get Barry McCartan?"

"Aye... I do, Commandant."

"And do you remember telling me that you could succeed with his son?"

Heaney's mouth was suddenly dry and he couldn't speak. He nodded and took a quick gulp. He was not used to drinking brandy and the burning liquid in his throat brought on a fit of coughing and choking.

"I'm sorry, sir," the humiliated butcher gasped, wiping tears from his eyes with his sleeve.

"Quite all right, Heaney. Just remember, brandy is to be sipped, not gulped."

"Yes, sir. I'll remember that, sir," he answered, knowing full well that he would probably never have another glass of brandy in his life.

"Concerning the Yank McCartan. I have a mission for you."

Heaney's mind was suddenly in turmoil. He was excited that the the squire was entrusting a mission to him. But what was expected of him?

"As you well know, Heaney, this McCartan from America has been a thorn in the side of all of us."

"Aye, that he has."

"Since the beginning of all this unpleasantness, I assumed that he would leave once he realized that he wasn't getting the answers he wanted. Well, it seems I was wrong. I believe he will persist in learning about his father. And that will mean that eventually he will learn the part you played in his father's life. I don't think you want that, do you?"

"No, sir, I do not." Nor would you, Squire, he thought to himself.

"So we've got to find a way to make him go away."

Heaney nodded.

"Do you know how we might do that?"

"I'm sure I don't, Squire."

Kerrigan stood up. "Another brandy?"

Heaney badly wanted another drink, but he was afraid he would choke on it again. "No, thank you, sir. That's enough for me."

Kerrigan poured himself another drink and sat back down.

Heaney, unable to stand the suspense any longer, blurted out, "Do you want me to kill him, Squire? Is that what you're asking of me?"

Kerrigan looked stricken. "Good lord, man. Nothing as desperate as all that."

"Then..."

"What I want you to do is frighten him in such a way that he will see the wisdom in returning to America straight away."

"And how would I do that, Squire?"

"I want you to... are you sure you wouldn't like another drink?"

The frightened Heaney held out his glass. He desperately needed another drink, and if he choked, so be it. "Aye, that would be grand, Squire."

Kerrigan handed him his brandy and sat back down. "Now, here is what I want you to do...."

~~

Matt came down to breakfast just after six. Karina glanced up at the wall clock. "You're up bright and early."

Matt made a face. "I need to talk to Hugh Cleary again."

"Uh-oh. Another ride in the dreaded currach?"

"Exactly."

"Sit down, I'll bring you a nice hearty breakfast."

Matt patted his stomach. "Just coffee. Bad enough I have to go on that damn boat, I don't want to get seasick and throw up."

She grinned. "Actually, that might be a good idea. You upchuck on his boat, maybe he won't let you back on board."

"I don't think it would matter. He's got this thing about not talking on solid ground."

When Karina came back with the coffee, he said, "By the way, where is that old couple? I haven't seen them in a couple of days."

"They finally realized the ancestors resided somewhere on the east coast. They left for Dublin yesterday."

"I envy them. I wish I could leave, too."

"Why?

"I don't know. I feel like I'm chasing my tail. That old priest Dunne is stonewalling me. Claire knows nothing about my father. Maeve can only tell me what she knows about him up to the day he went into Dingle. Kerrigan and my dad had a spat about the water rights, but for sure he's not about to talk to me about it. The only one who seems to know anything is an eccentric old guy who is determined to get me drowned."

Matt finished his coffee and stood up. "Wish me luck."

Karina glanced out the window and winced. Wind was whipping up whitecaps in the North Atlantic. "Luck. You're gonna need it."

~~

When Matt got down to the beach, he was dismayed to see four foot waves crashing on the beach and a sea foaming with whitecaps. His initial dread gave way to hope. With seas like that, surely Hugh wouldn't ask him to go out in these conditions.

When he got to the currach, Hugh was standing beside it studying the sea. Matt stood beside him and he, too, studied the sea. "Way too rough to go out today, right?" Matt said, hopefully.

"Ah, not a'tall. The only trouble with this wind is that it's hard to light my pipe. Give a hand here."

"Hugh, look at the size of these waves. We'll capsize. We'll drown."

"Not a'tall. Once we're past the breakers, it'll be calm as a lake, you'll see."

"I'm sorry. I can't do it."

Hugh squinted at him. "You came here to ask me more questions. Didn't you?"

"Yes."

"Well, then. Help me get the boat in the water, man."

The two previous times Matt had helped Hugh launch the boat, the sea had been calm and everything went smoothly. But now, as they shoved the boat into the surf, breaking waves jerked the bow to and fro, threatening to wrench the boat out of their hands.

"Get in," Hugh shouted over the wind and crashing waves. "Get in."

Matt dove into the boat and almost went out the other side. He tried to sit down, but it was like riding a bucking bronco. He grabbed the gunnels with both hands and held on. With an agility that belied his age, Hugh nimbly stepped into the boat. He grabbed the oars and began to row hard against the incoming sea. With the bow now pointed directly into the waves, the currach bit into the water and Hugh's powerful strokes drove the boat forward.

About a hundred yards off shore, the seas were much calmer. It was not like a lake, as Hugh had promised, but at least the crashing waves were behind them and the boat gently rose and fell with the rolling waves running beneath them.

Hugh put the oars down and took out his pipe. "Well, what is it you wanted to know?"

Matt decided to get right to the point. The quicker he got his answers, the quicker he could get back to shore. "Maeve said the last time she saw my father was the morning he, you, and that other fellow went into Dingle. You said after the ambush he went to hide in the mountains and to recover from his wound. How long was he in hiding?"

Hugh had a hard time lighting his pipe in the strong winds. After a long pause and several puffs, he said, "Well, you know it was a long time ago, but as I recall, it was about four weeks. Then, when he was well enough to travel, I went with him to Cork where he signed on as a deck hand for a ship going out to America."

Now Matt asked the troubling question that was constantly on his mind. "How come he never went back to see Maeve again? At least to say goodbye."

"Ah, that would be because of Father Dunne."

"What did he have to do with it?"

"While your da was hiding in the mountains, I had to bring him the bad news that Maeve was going to marry John Twomey."

"What was his reaction?"

"He was furious, he was. He said she would not marry that old man. He wanted to go to her at once, but I convinced him that it was too dangerous to show his face in the village."

"So where does Father Dunne come into this?"

"The night before the wedding was to take place, your da was beside himself, pacing and pacing. Against my advice, he said, damn all, he was going to see Dunne and tell him that he wanted to marry Maeve. And so he went."

Matt was stunned. That old priest flat out lied to his face when he claimed he couldn't remember Barry McCartan. "So what did Dunne say to him?"

"That I don't know. All I know is that when you da came back he was black sad, he was. I'd never seen him so down. I asked what had happened, but all he would say is that he was leaving for Cork in the morning and that was that."

"So you went to Cork with him and that was the last time you saw him?"

"Aye. He gave me an address where he would be staying with a friend in Brooklyn, New York. Later, I wrote him that Maeve had given birth to a baby girl." Hugh relit his pipe and after a long pause said, "And that was the last I heard of Barry McCartan."

Matt suddenly remembered the envelope marked Ballyturan he'd found in his father's suitcase. The envelope that started this whole crazy journey. "So it was you who wrote to my father?"

"Aye. Sure no one else knew where he'd gone."

Matt's head was spinning from these latest revelations. What could Father Dunne have said to him to make him abandon his pregnant girlfriend? Why wouldn't he allow them to marry? There was only one person who could answer those question. "Hugh, can you take me back now?"

The old man nodded and reached for the oars. Matt looked over his shoulder at a sight that terrified him. The rolling waves were crashing onto the beach with a wild ferocity. Getting out here had been bad enough. Getting in would be a lot worse.

But it wasn't as bad as he thought it would be. Hugh skillfully positioned the currach over a wave and surfed straight into the shore. The next thing Matt knew, Hugh was yelling for him to jump off and pull the boat up to the beach.

~~

Karina looked up from her book when Matt came rushing in. "Well, I see you survived another harrowing adventure on Hugh Cleary's currach."

"Yeah. Karina, is there some way you can get in touch with Maeve?"

"You're in luck. I'm going to a dance with Claire tonight. What do you need?"

"Tell her I have to see her again."

"Done."

~~

It was after eleven when Karina knocked on Matt's door. "Did I wake you?" she asked.

"No, come in. I'm wide awake."

She flopped down on the bed and Matt was suddenly aware of how attractive she was. Having her in his room at this hour, sitting on his bed, began to stir feelings in him. He felt like a fool and stammered, "Did… did you talk to Maeve?"

"Yep," she answered, seemingly unaware of the effect she was having on him. "She'll be on the beach at seven tomorrow morning."

"Thanks, Karina. I really appreciate all your help."

"Hey, it's my pleasure. It's not everyday a girl gets to play spy and courier in a sleepy village like Ballyturan. You've really livened up things since you've gotten here."

"Livened. That's one word for it. I think stirring up the pot would be the choice of Kerrigan and Dunne."

"Probably."

"Where did you go tonight?" he asked, realizing that he didn't want her to leave just yet.

"A dance over in the next village. You should have come. You're spending entirely too much time on your search. You know what they say, "All work and no play…""

"Makes Matt a dull boy. Hey, nobody invited me to the dance."

"Oh, I'm sorry. I will the next time. Promise."

She stood up. "Well, I gotta get some shuteye. My day starts early."

He opened the door and they stood awkwardly facing each other for a long moment. Then she leaned forward and gave him a hasty kiss on his cheek. "Good night."

"Yeah. Good night," he mumbled.

Chapter Sixteen

Matt got to the beach ten minutes before seven. A thick fog obscured the calm seas and the only sound was the soft lapping of water meeting the sand. It was damp and chilly. Matt pulled his zipped his jacket up, considering himself lucky. He could have been on his way to see Hugh and be forced to go on another traumatic fog-bound trip on his currach.

Out of the mist, he saw a dark shape coming toward him. Soon, Maeve was standing before him. "Good morning, Matt."

"Good morning, Maeve. Thank you for seeing me again."

"Karina said you seemed very anxious to see me."

"I am." It was a nasty morning and he didn't want to keep her here any longer than necessary. "Did you know my father went to see Dunne the night before your wedding?" he asked.

"Her eyes widened. "No, I did not. Father Dunne never mentioned it to me. Why would Barry go see him?"

"Well, according to Hugh Cleary, my father went to tell Dunne that he wanted to marry you."

At those words, Maeve's eyes filled with tears. "I didn't know that..." she said, turning away. After a moment to compose herself, she turned back to Matt. "I don't understand. If he wanted to marry me, why didn't he?"

"Apparently, Dunne talked him out of it."

"But why? Barry and l loved each other. We were going to have a child together. What could Father Dunne say that would make your father go away?"

"I don't know, but I'm going to find out. There's a novena tonight at the church. I'm going to confront him after the service and make him give me answers."

"I'll go with you," Maeve said firmly. "I'll be at the novena. When it's over, I'll go with you. I have some questions of my own."

"Are you sure?"

"I am. He had no right to withhold that information from me. All these years I thought... I thought..."

"You thought he'd abandoned you and Claire. That's what I thought, too." He saw her shiver and wondered was it due to the dampness or what he'd just told her. "You should be getting back. I'll see you tonight."

She touched his arm. "Aye. And, Matt thank you for telling me about Barry. It's cleared up so many troubling questions I've been asking myself all these years."

~~

It was almost nine when a small group of parishioners filed out of the church at the conclusion of the service. Matt stood across the road in the shadow of a stand of trees. Maeve was almost the last to come out. He crossed the road to join her.

"Maeve, are you sure you want to go through with this?"

"I am. The whole time I was in church, I was praying on it. It's the right thing to do."

"Okay. Let's go."

~~

Father Dunne opened the door and his eyes widened in surprise when he saw who it was. Ignoring Matt, he said to Maeve, "Maeve Twomey, what are you doing here this time of night?"

"We want to talk to you," Matt said.

"About what?"

"May we come in," Maeve asked.

The priest frowned. "It's terrible late. Come back tomorrow and..."

"No," Matt said decisively. "We have to talk now."

Matt's intimidating tone made the priest take a step back. Realizing they wouldn't go away, he said, "Very well. Come into my study. But I can't give you much time," he added brusquely.

As soon as they were seated, Matt, wasting no time, said, "Father Dunne, why did you lie to me when you said you didn't know my father?"

The abrupt question and accusatory tone caught the old priest off-guard. "Lie? Well, I wouldn't characterize it as a lie. You see... that is... I may have misspoke and..."

Matt cut him off. 'No, you deliberately lied to me and I want to know why."

The priest went on the offensive. "Now, see here, young man," he said, sternly. "I will not be spoken to in that tone of voice. I am the pastor of this church and a man of God ..."

"Dunne, I am not one of your cowering parishioners. I'm not even Catholic. You can't intimidate me by hiding behind your collar. By lying to me, you've forfeited the respect a true clergyman deserves."

Dunne fell back as though Matt had physically struck him. He realized now, too late, that he never should have let them in. He needed time to prepare himself. He needed time to consult with Kerrigan to determine how he should respond to these inflammatory questions.

Matt had noticed that up until now, Maeve had said nothing. He'd made the crack about "cowering parishioners" for her benefit. He wanted her to know she didn't have to be one of those people.

Apparently, Maeve got the message. She leaned forward and in a soft, but strong voice, said, "Father, Barry McCartan came to see you the night before my wedding to John Twomey. I want to know what was said at that meeting."

The old priest stared at her blankly. How in the world could she know that? "Who told you that?" he snapped.

"That's not important," Matt said. "Just answer the question."

"I cannot... I will not divulge what was said," Dunne sputtered. Then in desperation, he added, "I will not break the solemn oath of the confessional."

"Come off it, Dunne," Matt said. "My father didn't come to you for the forgiveness of his sins. He came to tell you he wanted to marry Maeve. What did you say to him that made him change his mind?"

Defeated, the old priest seemed to deflate before their eyes. The haughtiness left him and the air of authority vanished, leaving only an old pathetic man who had many sins to account for. He rubbed his hands together in anguish and dropped his eyes to avoid Maeve's steady, accusatory gaze.

"You have to remember," he began slowly, in a soft voice, "it was a long time ago... It was the time of the uprising. The whole country was in turmoil. There was death and treachery everywhere. When young Maeve, pregnant with child, and her mother came to me to ask my advice about what to..."

"Excuse me, Father," Maeve interrupted. "I didn't come to you for advice. It was you who sent for me and my mother."

He waved a hand in dismissal. "Whatever. I won't quibble over words. The point is, I advised you to marry John Twomey and good advice it was. Didn't John give you and your child a fine life with a roof over your heads and food on the table?"

"We know all that," Matt said, impatiently. "Tell us what took place the night my father came to see you."

A flash of anger crossed Dunne's face and he seemed to change yet again. His face took on a belligerent cast. "He almost ruined everything, he did." And the words poured out of him. "What right did he have to come to talk about marriage the night before the wedding that had already been planned out? Hadn't the banns been read from the altar for three Sundays? What right did he, a man with a price on his head, to think he could take on the responsibility for a young mother and child? And what about the new roof for the church? Don't you see, it was a condition of the marriage. If there was no marriage, there would be no roof. I needed that roof. The bishop was so proud when I told him a parishioner had donated the money and it would cost the church nothing. He said that in that case, the church would stay open. That was a glorious day…."

The words had flowed out of him in a torrent of self-pity. Matt got the impression that he was talking more to himself than to them and that he was trying to convince himself that his actions were right and proper.

He looked up at them in surprise, as though he'd forgotten they were there. "I ask you," he went on, "how do you weigh all that against one man's ill-advised wish to marry? Of course, none of what I said swayed him. He was obstinate, he was. Can you believe he told me that none of that mattered? That the only thing that mattered was that he and Maeve were in love? Pure foolishness. Still, I was desperate. I had to find a way for him to see the folly of his ways. And thanks be to God I finally thought of a way to convince him. I told him that he was wrong about Maeve. I told him she didn't love him. How could she after he had abandoned her in her hour of need? God help me, I told him Maeve wanted to marry John Twomey so that she could raise her child in peace and prosperity. I told him that if he really loved Maeve, he would get out of her life and never have anything more to do with her." He looked from Maeve to Matt beseechingly. "It was the right thing to do. Don't you see that?"

He wanted understanding, but when he got no response, his lower lip trembled and he began to weep. "God forgive me…" he muttered. "I was only trying to do what was right. That's all I was trying to do…." His voice trailed off.

Maeve and Matt were stunned into silence by Dunne's confession. The enormity of what this incredibly foolish man had done was beyond comprehension. Whether because of greed, or self-aggrandizement, he had altered and damaged all their lives. He seemed to have no idea of the human wreckage he'd caused.

Maeve began to weep. At first, quietly, but soon her whole body was racked with sobs. Tears welled up in Matt's eyes as well. But mostly, he wanted to reach across the desk and slap that stupid old man. He took Maeve's hand. "Do you have any more questions?" he asked gently.

She shook her head, too distraught to speak.

He stood up. "Then that's it." He looked at Dunne with contempt. "God have mercy on your soul. I hope he can forgive you your sins, because I sure as hell can't." He took Maeve's arm. "Come on. We're done here."

106

As they started for the door, Dunne, his eyes filled with tears and his voice breaking with emotion, called out, "Wait. Maeve Twomey, I… I have something for you…"

Wiping away the tears with his sleeve, he opened his desk drawer, rummaged through its contents and produced an envelope. It was yellowed with age and reminded Matt of the envelope he'd found in his father's suitcase.

"I should have given it to you a long time ago, but I…" he shrugged helplessly and offered it to Maeve.

Maeve took the envelope and looked at the single word written— Maeve—and sucked in her breath. "My God, this is Barry's handwriting…" she whispered. She sunk into a chair and opened the envelope. Inside was a single page, yellowed with age. She read in silence.

> *My Dearest, Dearest Maeve,*
> *I write this letter in Father Dunne's study. First and foremost I want to say that I love you beyond all understanding and I always have and always will. I freely admit that I have not met my obligations to you, or our child, in a timely manner. And for that, I beg your forgiveness. I should have heeded your warnings. I never should have gone off with the Volunteers that fateful day. You tried to warn me, but I was callow and stupid and, now I realize, easily swayed. But that is all in the past and what's done is done. Also, I should not have gone into Dingle that day. Our lives might have been different if I hadn't. But, again, it's no use dwelling on what might have been.*
> *I came to the rectory tonight to tell Father Dunne that I wanted to marry you, but he has convinced me that the best thing I can do for you and our unborn child is to be out of your lives forever. He has told me that you no longer love me and that you want to marry John Twomey for the sake of yourself and our child. Although it breaks my heart to hear that, I fully understand and accept it. You and our baby deserve to have the best in life.*
> *Reluctantly, I must agree with Father Dunne. The best thing I can do for you and our child is to separate myself from your lives. And so I will. Tomorrow morning, I am off to Cork where I will board a ship for America. I*

don't know what my future life will be like, but I wish you
and our unborn child every happiness.
Love forever,
Barry

With tears streaming down her cheeks, Maeve carefully folded up the letter and put it back in the envelope. "I want to go home now," she said quietly.

Without a word or nod to the weeping old priest, Maeve and Matt walked out of the rectory.

~~

Outside, Matt took her by the arm, trouble by the expression on her face. "Are you okay?"

"Yes... no... Oh, I don't know what to think. I guess I'm just overwhelmed. It's going to take a while to digest all that I heard and read in the letter tonight."

"Yeah. It was shock to me, too. But it's a relief to know that my father was an honorable man after all." He didn't know what was in the letter and he didn't want to read it. That was something personal between Maeve and his father. He shook his head. "I can't believe that old bastard Dunne didn't give you the letter sooner. And I can't believe he did what he did for a goddamn roof."

"That's something I'm sure he's had to live with his whole life." Maeve kissed Matt's cheek. "Thank you for everything, Matt."

"For what? I didn't do anything."

"You did. You know I was angry about you coming to Ballyturan. And I resented you for wanting to dredge up all those painful memories that I had been trying to repress for years. But I'm glad you came. By coming here to Ballyturan, you were able to uncover the truth that has eluded me all these years. If you hadn't come, I never would have know the real reason Barry went away. It's a comfort to know that he loved me and he just wanted the best for me and Claire."

"Will you show her the letter?"

"Yes. I think it will be a comfort to her as well to know the reason why she grew up without her real father." She wrapped her shawl tightly around her. "Well, I'm off to home."

"I'll walk with you."

"There's no need."

"Please. I want to."

He took her arm and in silence they walked the dark road to the farm, each reflecting on what they'd heard tonight. When they came to the farm gate, Matt stopped. "I think you can make it from here."

"Aye, I believe I can. Goodnight, Matt."

"Goodnight, Maeve."

When Maeve came into the house, Claire was siting by the fire reading. She looked up and frowned. "Mum, what's wrong? You look like you've seen a ghost."

Maeve's smile was sad. "In a way, I guess you could say I have."

"I don't understand."

Maeve handed her the letter. "I think you should read this."

Chapter Seventeen

Matt was halfway back to Ballyturan when he saw a man coming up the road toward him. He took no notice until, as he neared, Matt realized that the man had a handkerchief covering his face. Then he pulled out a a gun and pointed it at him.

"Stand where you are," the man shouted.

At first, Matt thought it was Kerrigan's man, the one who had pointed the shotgun at him. But this man was shorter and not as beefy. Then a crazy thought came into his head—could it be a Dublin assassin coming to finish the job they failed with his father?

Matt took a step forward. "What do you want? Is this a robbery?"

"Don't come any nearer, I'm warning you."

Matt's combat instincts kicked in and all his senses became sharp and focused. He noticed the hand holding the gun was shaking and his voice was high-pitched with fear. This was no professional assassin.

"You're to leave Ballyturan at dawn tomorrow, if you know what's good for you."

Matt took another step. "And if I don't?"

The gunman hesitated, as though he hadn't expected that response. "There'll be consequences. I can tell you that."

Matt took another step. "If it's money you want, I can give it to you in pounds. Or if you prefer, I have American dollars. That's probably worth more than pounds. What do you think? Which would you prefer?" He hoped his talking would distract the man and it was working. The gunman didn't realize Matt was closing on him. He took one more step. Now he was in range.

"I don't want your money, McCartan. I'm telling you, you're to—"

He never got a chance to finish the sentence. As Matt lunged, he scooped up a handful of dirt and flung it in the man's face. When he put his hand up to clear his eyes, Matt grabbed the pistol with both hands and twisted it violently. He heard the satisfying crack of bone as the man howled in pain. He kneed the gunman in the groin and he collapsed in the roadway writhing in pain. "Jaysus! My wrist... you've broken my wrist..."

Matt straddled his chest and pointed the pistol in his face. "Who are you?"

"Heaney... Brian Heaney.... For the love of God, please don't kill me."

Matt yanked the handkerchief from his face. "You're the butcher."

"Aye."

"Who sent you."

"I... I can't tell you that."

"How do you know my name?"

"Would you get off me chest for Jaysus sake. I can hardly breathe."

Matt examined the pistol and recognized it as a very old Webley revolver, which at one time had been standard issue for the British Army. He broke the top action and six bullets ejected. From the condition of the old pistol, he doubted it was capable of being fired. He pretended to put one round in the chamber and closed it.

"Heaney, do you know what Russian roulette is?"

The terrified man shook his head.

"I've just loaded one round into this pistol. Every time you lie to me, I pull the trigger. Every time I pull the trigger, you have one chance in six of dying." He placed the muzzle against Heaney's forehead. "I'll ask you again. Who sent you?"

"I... I can't tell you that..."

Matt pulled the trigger and Heaney shrieked at the sound of the click. "Jaysus, Mary and Joseph... are you going to murder me?"

"That's up to you. Who sent you?"

"I can't..."

Matt spun the chamber and pulled the trigger. Another click. Heaney howled in terror. Please... for the love of God...."

"Who sent you?"

"Wait... wait. Don't pull the trigger again... I'll tell you..."

Matt climbed off him and made him kneel in the middle of the road. "Who sent you?"

"It was the Squire. Squire Kerrigan."

Matt was taken aback. Did Kerrigan know he discovered he owned the farm? Would he really send someone to kill him for that? "Did he send you to kill me?"

"No, no. Nothing like that. I was to scare you, that's all. So that you would leave town and not cause anymore trouble. Can I get up now? Me back is killing me and my wrist..."

"No. Stay where you are." During the war this position was the standard operating procedure when interrogating a prisoner. A kneeling man is a vulnerable man. And a vulnerable man is more likely to talk.

"Why did Kerrigan pick you for this job?" If he was supposed to frighten me, Matt thought, he picked the wrong guy.

"I was a soldier in the Volunteers. Squire Kerrigan was my commandant."

Matt was puzzled. "Are the Volunteers still active?"

"No, but... I'm still a soldier nonetheless."

"If you fought back in sixteen, you must have known my father."

Heaney hesitated. "I don't think so."

Matt jammed the pistol's barrel into Heaney's mouth. "You're a lying sonofabitch. The first day I came into Ballyturan, you saw me looking in the window of your shop and you reacted like you'd just seen a ghost. I reminded you of my father. Isn't that right?"

"All right, all right. Now I remember. Yes, we were in the Dublin Post Office together. But there were a lot of other men there as well. It's hard to remember everyone."

"Who accused my father of being an informer?"

Heaney's lower lip trembled and he looked away. "I'm sure I don't know anything about that," he stammered.

Matt had a feeling that Heaney was withholding something from him, but he couldn't figure out what it was. "All right, on your feet."

Heaney gratefully stood up, holding his broken wrist. "Can I go now, sir?"

"Yeah. And you can tell Squire Kerrigan that I have no intention of leaving town."

"I'll tell him that, sir. I will." Grateful to still be alive, Heaney turned and scurried back up the road.

Matt put the six rounds back in pistol and pulled the trigger six times. It was as he suspected. The firing pin was broken. The gun was incapable of being fired. He shoved the pistol in his belt and watched the frightened man go, wondering if he had any connection to the men who had tried to kill his father. There was only one man in Ballyturan who could answer that question.

~~

Kerrigan glared at Heaney, barely able to contain his rage. There would be no offer to sit down; no offer of a drink this time. "So he took your pistol away from you?"

Heaney held up his arm. "He broke my wrist, he did. He's powerful strong. There was nothing I could do."

"And you told him I sent you?"

"He was going to kill me if I didn't answer his questions. He had the pistol to my head the entire time."

"What did he say when you told him to leave Ballyturan?"

"He said to tell you that he's not going anywhere."

Kerrigan turned away from the pathetic man in disgust. "All right. Off with you."

"Yes. Goodnight, Commandant."

A livid Kerrigan poured himself a brandy. He realized now it had been a mistake sending Heaney to confront McCartan. In his heart of hearts, he knew McCartan wouldn't back down so easily. Although he wouldn't admit it to himself, he had half-hoped Heaney would panic and actually shoot the Yank. That would have solved a lot of his problems. Now he would just have to wait to see what McCartan's next move would be.

~~

As Matt hurried along the beach toward Hugh's cottage, he glanced at his watch; it was almost eleven. At least, he thought with some relief, Hugh couldn't drag him out on that damn currach in the dark. He climbed the hill and knocked on the door. He heard some shuffling and then the door opened. A sleepy Hugh squinted at Matt.

"'Tis the middle of the night. What are you doing here?"

"I have some questions."

"Come back tomorrow. We'll go on the boat."

He started to close the door, but Matt blocked it with his foot. "Less than an hour ago, a man named Heaney tried to kill me."

Hugh squinted at him in silence. For a dreaded second, Matt thought he was going to say they would have to go on the boat. Instead, he said, "Come in. Come in."

The cottage was tiny to begin with, but crammed as it was the years of accumulated flotsam and jetsam that Hugh had retrieved from the sea and the beach, there was barely a place to sit down. He swept an old fishing net off a chair. "Have a seat and tell me what is it that you want to know."

"Who is Heaney and what's his relation to Kerrigan?"

Matt waited patiently while Hugh lit up his pipe. "During the uprising, Squire Kerrigan was our commandant. Heaney was just another soldier, and a bad one at that."

"Why do you say that?"

"He liked to think he was a tough soldier, but the man was a craven coward. When they took us off to the prison, he cried like a baby, he did. I never trusted him." Hugh took the pipe out of his mouth and stared at it for a long while. "There was talk it was Brian Heaney who testified against you da," he said softly.

"What? He told me he barely knew my father."

"He's lying."

"Why would he lie about my father?"

"I don't know the answer to that question. There was an informer. We all knew that because the soldiers came and arrested Volunteers who weren't at the Post Office. They also knew exactly where we had hidden weapons and explosives. There was an informer among us, but it wasn't your da."

Matt stood up. "Where does Heaney live?"

"In the back of his shop."

"Is he married?"

"His wife left him years ago. Took their only child with her, too."

"So he lives there alone."

"Aye. Where are you off to now?"

"To pay a visit to the butcher."

"At this time of night? You Yanks keep terrible hours you do."

~~

Matt peered into the window of the butcher shop. The lights were out and there was no sign of anyone home. He started to walk around to the back of the shop, when he saw a figure hurrying down the street. It was Heaney. Matt stepped into a darkened doorway and watched as the butcher fumbled for his keys. As soon as he opened the door, Matt charged, knocking the terrified man into the store and sprawling onto the floor.

"Jaysus, Mary, and Saint Joseph..." Heaney said, scrambling to his feet. "Is it you again?"

Matt pointed the gun at Heaney. "Yeah, and the game is still on."

"For the love of God, haven't I told you everything I know?"

"What you told me was lies. You said you barely knew my father, but it was you who testified against him."

Heaney paled. "But how did you know..." He caught himself and muttered indignantly, "I did no such a thing."

Matt pointed the pistol at Heaney's face and pulled the trigger.

Heaney howled in fright and fell back into a chair. "Please... please don't shoot me dead..."

Matt Yanked him out of the chair and forced him into a kneeling position. "Heaney," he snarled at the petrified butcher, "you're going to tell me everything you know or I swear to Christ this will be your last night on earth."

Heaney began to sob and blubber. "I don't want to die... Please... please..."

"Why did you testify against my father?"

When Heaney hesitated, Matt put the pistol to his forehead. "Remember, you have a one in six chance of dying."

"It was Twomey," he blurted out. "It was John Twomey who made me do it."

114

"Twomey? What's he got to do with it?"

"There was an informer back then. We all knew that. But no one knew who. One day, Twomey came to see me. At the time I was working for old Peter Cahill, the owner of the butcher shop. Twomey said he had a proposition for me. If I would testify against your da, if I would say I'd witnessed him informing to the Brits while we were in the prison, he would lend me the money to buy out old man Cahill. I didn't want to do it. I knew it wasn't right. But it was the chance of a lifetime it was. Cahill wanted to sell the shop, but I hadn't the money to buy it. If he sold it to someone else, there was a good chance I would be out of a job. And where would that leave me, I ask you?"

Matt was speechless with rage. Heaney had framed his father and now he was asking for sympathy and understanding. He was grateful the pistol's firing pin was broken or he might have shot Heaney dead right then and there. Taking a deep breath to bring his anger under control, he said, "Why would Twomey want you to testify against my father?"

"Because he was sweet on Maeve. He wanted to marry her himself. He thought if your da was out of the way..." Heaney finished the sentence with a helpless shrug.

Matt could scarcely believe what he was hearing. Twomey was at least twenty-five years older than Maeve. How could he possibly think he could get her to marry him? Then the answer hit him—money. He'd pulled it off by first bribing Heaney to testify against his father, and then by bribing Father Dunne to convince Maeve to marry him.

The butcher was now sobbing uncontrollably. Matt grabbed him by the hair and yanked his face up. He put the pistol to Heaney's forehead. "I have one more question for you. I know you know who the real informer was. Who was it?"

The broken man gasped for air. "It was me..." he whispered.

"*You?*"

"They tortured me they did. They made me stand at attention all night. They slapped me. They hit me with truncheons. They said they would kill me and make it look like an accident. I had no choice. I had to tell them what they wanted to know. I had to. When Twomey made me his offer, I didn't do it for the money. Well, at least not at first. I was terrified that someone would find out it was me who was the informer. By testifying against your da, it took all suspicion away from me." He suddenly realized he'd said too much. "I'm so sorry I did it," he added by way of contrition. "I've not had a decent night's sleep ever since."

Matt felt those unwelcome murderous combat instincts welling up in him again. And he knew—Heaney would have to die for what he'd done. Almost blind with rage, Matt said, "Stand up." When the butcher did as he was told, Matt put his hands around Heaney's throat and began to choke him. Heaney's eyes bulged and he grunted like a wild animal as he struggled to be free of Matt's iron grasp. Suddenly, Matt let go of him. He couldn't do it. He'd done enough killing in the war. He was sick of it all. He looked at the gasping man for a moment and then slapped him hard across the face. "If you were a real man, I would kill you. But you're a coward and a liar and you're not worth going to jail for."

Matt stormed out of the shop, leaving the broken Heaney standing there, terrified, but relieved he was still alive.

~~

Matt stumbled down to the beach, hoping the night air and the sea breezes would clear his head and calm his troubled soul. As he walked, his rage slowly subsided. He shuddered at the thought that he'd come close to strangling Heaney earlier.

Hugh had been right about the butcher. He was a coward. He imagined the British Army at that time, in one way or another, tortured all their prisoners. But it was only Heaney who cracked. If his actions hadn't been so devastating to the lives of his father and Maeve, he would have thought the man more to be pitied than scorned.

As for his father, it seemed inconceivable that that taciturn man he grew up with could have gone through all this. It was no wonder he never wanted to talk about Ireland or his past. As he walked up the path to the road, he realized that it was Twomey who was the real cause of all this. But what would he do about him? He didn't know the answer to that question.

~~

By the time Matt got back to the hotel, it was almost one in the morning, but Karina was still up. "Where were you? I was beginning to worry."

"I need a drink."

She studied his face. "Yeah, I think you do."

Over drinks, he told her about the events of the night. When he was finished, she shook her head in amazement. "Wow. And all this time I thought Ballyturan was this little sleepy village. So what's next?"

"Tomorrow I'm going to have a go around with Kerrigan. But I still don't know what to do about Twomey."

"You have to confront him too, don't you?"

"I certainly want to, but I don't know how Maeve will react when she finds out that the man she's been married to all these years had tricked her and destroyed her chance for happiness with my father."

"Yeah, I see your point." "I can't get over the fact that Dunne, Kerrigan, Twomey, and Heaney for their own selfish reasons wrecked my father and Maeve's lives."

"And what about you?"

"What do you mean?"

"You said you didn't have a great relationship with your father. Don't you think they bear responsibility for that as well?"

Matt was silent for a moment. "I hadn't thought of that, but you're right. Because of what they did to him, I was raised by a broken, disengaged man whose dreams of happiness had been ripped away from him." Tears welled up in his eyes. "Those sonsofbitches deprived me of a real father."

Karina put her arms around him, and she, too, began to weep. "I'm so sorry, Matt..." She looked up at him and they kissed. Neither was surprised. It seemed like the most natural thing in the world to both of them. Matt brushed a tear from her cheek and smiled. "I just thought of something ironic. If everything had gone the way Barry and Maeve planned, I would never have been born."

She kissed him again. "Well, I for one am very glad you were born."

Chapter Eighteen

After a sleepless night, Matt came down to breakfast. Karina came out of the kitchen with a pot of coffee. "Full breakfast?"

Matt made a face. "I'm too wound up to eat. Just coffee."

She poured the coffee and sat down across from him. "So what's your game plan?"

"I don't have one." He pushed the cup away from him and stood up. "I can't drink that right now. Wish me luck."

She kissed him and whispered, "Luck."

~~

Matt left Karina's bike at the side of the road. When he walked up the lane to what was now his farm, he saw Kerrigan and several of his men milling about watching a herd of cattle drinking from his pond. The sight of Kerrigan trespassing on his land infuriated him, especially since that arrogant bastard had driven him off his land only a few days ago. He was relieved to see that no one was carrying a shotgun.

Kerrigan saw a determined McCartan coming up the lane and had an immediate flashback of the day the young Yank's father had stood at the bottom of his terrace steps and challenged him over the water rights. Was this to be repeated?

"What is it you want?" Kerrigan called out.

"I want you to get your cattle off my land. Right now."

One of the men made a move toward Matt, but Kerrigan put a restraining hand on him. "All right, men. Take the cattle back to the fields."

Matt was taken aback by the sudden surrender. He didn't think Kerrigan would give up so easily. He half-expected he would have to fight one—or all—of Kerrigan's men. He watched with folded arms as the puzzled herdsmen, shooting sharp glances at him, did as they were told. When the last of the cattle had been driven away, only Kerrigan and Matt remained.

And that's the way Kerrigan wanted it. He wasn't sure what would happen next, but clearly the Yank had the upper hand and he didn't want his men to witness that. The old squire studied the Yank carefully. Since he'd found out that McCartan knew he owned the farm, he had contemplated stonewalling him and forcing him to bring in a solicitor. But in the end, he decided it was no use. The last thing he wanted was for this issue of farm ownership to come into a public forum. It would not go well for him or his reputation. There was a better way. He'd spend all his adult life making deals and negotiating with men much shrewder than this callow Yank. They both knew the farm belonged to him. There was no dispute there. He was pretty sure the Yank had no intention of farming the land himself, so this was going to be about money.

Kerrigan stepped up to Matt. "We have to come to an arrangement, McCartan."

"What's your offer?"

"I'll pay you a reasonable fee for use of the water rights."

"What about all those years you've been using the pond? Are you prepared to pay back fees for all those years?"

"Ach, man," Kerrigan snapped, "that was a long time ago. Let's just talk about the present."

"Nope. I want to talk about how you are going to compensate me for using the pond all those years."

Kerrigan glared at Matt, regretting his decision to give in so easily. The Yank was just like his father—stubborn and prideful and unwilling to listen to reason. "All right, all right. I'll pay you a hundred pounds for past rights."

Matt chuckled. "You can't be serious. That's not even four pounds a year. Unacceptable."

"Then what is it that you want?" the squire asked in exasperation.

"I told you. You'll pay me the standard fees for past use and you'll pay me the standard fees for future use. Or," Matt hesitated for a moment, "you can buy the farm."

Kerrigan shook his head vehemently. "Sure the farm is nothing more than a hopeless pile of dirt. It's only the water I want."

"That's my offer, Kerrigan. Take it or leave it."

Kerrigan saw he was running out of options. To buy some time he said, "Have your solicitor draw up an offer and I'll look at it."

"Okay. But, starting today, if you want to continue using my water, you'll pay the standard fee. Is that understood?"

Kerrigan's face reddened. He wasn't accustomed to having anyone talk to him in that tone of voice. He wanted to tell him to go to hell or go back to America or—but he had his livestock to think about. "Done," he muttered, turning on his heels and walking away.

~~

Matt had intended to ride back to Ballyturan and then continue on to Dingle to see Mr. O'Doherty, but instead, he turned around and headed for the Twomey farm. What was to be done with the farm was not solely his decision to make. Claire was half owner. She should also have a say.

Maeve had warned him not to come to the farm, but after what he'd found out about Twomey, he really didn't care what Twomey would like or not like. He turned onto the lane leading to the farm and saw the old man plowing a field at the base of a hill half a mile away. It didn't matter to him if he had a confrontation with the old man or not, but it would be best for Maeve and Claire if there was no unpleasantness.

A wide-eyed Maeve opened the door to his knock. "Matt," she said, looking over his shoulder, as though John Twomey might be standing there, "what are you doing here? You shouldn't have come."

"It's important, Maeve. Is Claire here?"

"Yes, come in. Come in," she said, quickly slamming the door.

Hearing voices, Claire came out of her room. She gave him that same wide-eyed look. "Matt, you shouldn't..."

"I know. But I had to see you right away. May I sit down?"

Maeve motioned to a seat at the table. "Of course, please sit down. I'll make some tea."

"What is this all about," Claire asked.

"Let me get right to the point. Kerrigan doesn't own our father's farm."

Maeve turned away from the stove with a quizzical expression. "I don't understand. Everyone in Ballyturan knows..."

"He's been lying all these years. He needed the water for his livestock. There was no way my father could, or would have, sold him the farm, so he just took it and pretended he bought it."

"How do you know all this?" Claire asked.

"I went to Dingle and hired a solicitor to research the land deeds."

"So who does own the farm?"

"You and me."

Claire jerked her head back in astonishment. " You.... me? How can that be?"

"The deed is still in the name of Barry McCartan. There are only two heirs and that's you and me."

"My God... I don't know what to say."

"I'm on my way to see the solicitor. I want you to come to Dingle with me."

"What ever for?"

"As co-owners we have to decide what to do with the farm."

Claire held her head in her hands. "I'm overwhelmed. I don't know what to say."

"Don't look so worried, Claire, you're a landowner. That's good, isn't it?"

"I suppose… still…" She looked at her mother. "What should I do, Mum?"

Maeve brought three mugs to the table and sat down. "Well, this is an astonishing bit of news…" After a moment, she said, "I think you should go with Matt."

~~

After they finished their tea, Matt and Claire rode their bikes back to the hotel. As soon as they came through the door, Karina jumped up and hugged Claire.

"Have you heard the news?" Claire asked.

Karina shot a quizzical glance at Matt, looking for a cue as to what she should say. Was Claire talking about the terrible thing that John Twomey had done, or was it about the farm?

"She means that she and I own the farm," Matt said.

"Oh, yes. Matt told me. That's wonderful news."

"We'll grab a bite to eat and then we're going into Dingle to see O'Doherty."

"On those two rickety bicycles? No dice. I'll call a liveryman to drive you."

By the time they finished eating, the liveryman was outside, honking his horn.

~~

The driver, an earnest young man with a protruding Adam's apple, took his cap off. "Good day to you, sir. My name is James Casey and I have the pleasure of driving you to Dingle."

He was a pleasant enough fellow but he couldn't stop asking questions about America once he found out Matt was from there. He was mildly annoying, but Matt had to admit that the ride to Dingle was a lot faster and a lot safer than on a bicycle dodging sheep, goats, and cows.

The car pulled up in front of O'Doherty's office. "Here we are," the liveryman announced. "Do you want me to wait for you?"

"Yes. If that's no trouble."

"No trouble at all. I have so many more questions to ask you about America."

"Great. I can't wait," Matt said, rolling his eyes at Claire.

When they came into the solicitor's office, they found him seated behind his paper strewn desk.

"Ah, good day to you Mr. McCartan," he said, standing up. "It's a pleasure to see you again."

"Mr. O'Doherty. I'd like to introduce my sister, Claire Twomey."

O'Doherty formally shook hands. "And it's a pleasure to meet you, Miss Twomey. Please be seated and tell me how I may I be of service to you."

"The last time I was here you told me there was some paperwork that had to be filed with the court."

"Indeed. It's a mere formality, but it must be done. By the way, how did your meeting with Squire Kerrigan go?"

"Better than expected. Kerrigan didn't put up a fight. He admitted we own the farm. Now, Claire and I have to decide what to do with it."

"Of course. Do either of you intent to farm the land?"

Matt looked at Claire. "Not me. How about you?"

"Absolutely not," she said, astonished at the very thought.

"Then is it your intention to rent out the farm?" O'Doherty asked.

"There's a problem there," Matt said. "Kerrigan is balking at paying the standard rate for the water rights and he only offered me a hundred pounds for the past thirty years of use."

O'Doherty chuckled mirthlessly. "That's the squire for you. Always looking to shape a deal in his favor."

"Besides that, I don't trust him," Matt continued. "What if a year from now he reneges on the payments? I'm going back to the states and I don't think Claire is going to want to deal with that."

"I certainly do not," Claire said firmly.

"Well, then it sounds like the best course of action is to sell the farm to him—or someone else."

"Would anyone else buy it?" Claire asked.

O'Doherty opened a folder, studied the land report, and frowned. "Not likely I'm afraid. It's a small farm and the soil is very poor. In the current economic climate one would be hard pressed to eke out a living on it."

"So where do we go from here?" Matt asked.

O'Doherty took off his glasses and rubbed them with his handkerchief. "Let me draw up a pair of contracts for the squire. He's a hard negotiator, but," he added with a twinkle in his eye, "I'm no slouch in that department myself." He stood up. "I'll telephone the hotel when everything is in readiness."

~~

The hired car pulled up at the lane leading to the Twomey farm. As Matt opened the door for Claire, they saw an angry Twomey stomping down the lane towards them.

"Oh, my," Claire said, her eyes widening in fright.

As Twomey came up to them, he looked as though he might strike Claire. Matt stepped between them. Knowing all the harm this foolish old man had caused, it took all the restraint he could marshal to keep from punching him. Instead, he said, "You have something to say, say it to me."

"I have nothing to say to you, Yank."

He tried to push past Matt, but Matt grabbed him by the shirt. He tried to pull away and Matt was surprised at how strong he was. Matt leaned in close and whispered, "Listen, Twomey, soon you and I are going to have a conversation about the new roof for Dunne's church." An astonished Twomey staggered backwards. Still holding on to his shirt, Matt said, "In the meantime, if you lay a finger on Maeve or Claire, I will come after you."

Twomey looked from Matt to Claire, and then in frustration stomped off toward the field where his horse was patiently grazing.

Claire watched him go in amazement. "What did you say to him?"

"I told him to act like a gentleman."

She suspected it was more than that, but she let it go. "I guess I should tell my Mum what's happening."

"Good idea."

"What about old John?"

"It doesn't matter if he knows." He'll have plenty to answer for when I confront him about his loan to the butcher, Matt said to himself with some satisfaction.

~~

It was after five in the afternoon when Twomey pounded on the door of the rectory. Nora opened the door and he practically bowled her over in his haste to get into Father Dunne's study.

"Here, here," Dunne said, looking up from his missal when Twomey came bursting in. "What's this?"

"What did you tell McCartan?" Twomey bellowed.

Dunne took his glasses off and calmly laid them on the desk. "You can go now," he said to the outraged Nora, who was standing in the doorway breathing heavily and glaring at Twomey.

"What is it that you want, Twomey?"

"I want to know what you told McCartan about our secret deal over the roof. You had no right to reveal that sacred trust."

"Come, come, man. That deal was not protected by the confessional and you know it."

"Nonetheless, that was a deal between you and me. What did you tell him?"

"The truth," Dunne shouted, losing his patience with the querulous farmer. "Something I have neglected to do for far too long."

"Well, what am I to do now?" Twomey asked.

"You'll have to defend your own actions, won't you? It's not the end of the world, man. Whatever your motives, paying for a new roof for the church was a charitable act for which God will bless you."

"Ach, that's easy for you to say," Twomey hissed, turning on his heels and stomping out of the study.

Dunne got up wearily from his chair and knelt down, blessed himself and leaned his elbows on the chair. Tears streamed down his cheeks. "Lord God in heaven…" he whispered, "please forgive this sinner, now and at the hour of my death. Amen."

~~

The next morning, Matt headed off to the beach to see Hugh. For a change, he had no questions; it was he who had the answers. He found Hugh squatting by the upturned currach cleaning his catch.

"Good morning, Hugh."

The fisherman looked up. "And good morning to you. Have you more questions for me?"

"No. I came to answer a few questions you might have been asking yourself over the years."

Hugh took out his pipe and began to fill it with tobacco. "Well, sit down, man. Sit down."

When Matt finished telling him what had transpired over the past few days, there were tears in Hugh's eyes. "I never trusted that Heaney. Not for a moment. And although I had my suspicions, I never thought he would stoop to do such a thing. His lies put a death sentence on you da's head. And Twomey, there are no words to describe the sorrow he caused all of you." Hugh shook his head and stared out to sea. "You once asked me why I live like a hermit."

"I did, and I'm sorry. It was none of my business."

"No, it was a fair question. After all that business—the shooting at the crossroads, your da going away, Maeve marrying that bugger Twomey—I was angry at the world. Your da didn't deserve that. Maeve didn't deserve that. And I felt great sorrow at your da's leaving. We had been best of friends since we were wee youngsters. And I felt disgust with myself. I should have spoken up in defense of your da, but the truth is"— he paused and stared at the fish in the bucket—"I was afraid. The Volunteers were a murderous bunch. I was afraid they would come for me as well."

Matt was touched. This was the first time since he'd met him that Hugh had displayed any emotion. And he was touched by the depth of his feeling for his father. "You had a right to be afraid, Hugh," he said gently. "Those were turbulent times. They tried to kill my father and I'm sure they wouldn't have hesitated to kill you if they thought it necessary."

Hugh shrugged. "Be that as it may, I became disgusted with the lot of them—Dunne, Kerrigan, Heaney, and Twomey, and everyone else in the village. For a time there, I even considered taking my own life." He waved his hand toward the sea. "It would have been so easy to take the currach out a few miles and jump overboard. I don't know how to swim so that would have been that."

Matt didn't know which was more startling—that he thought about killing himself, or that he couldn't swim. He couldn't imagine anyone going out in that flimsy boat day after day on to that unforgiving and violent sea and not knowing how to swim.

"It turned out I was too much of a coward to kill myself and so I became a hermit of sorts. Fishing all day and once a week selling my catch on market day."

After an awkward silence, Matt said, "Well, I'd better be going."

Hugh picked a fish out of the bucket. "Aye." And without another word he began to gut the fish.

When Matt got back to the hotel, Karina met him at the door. "O'Doherty called. He's set up a meeting with Kerrigan for tomorrow morning. He'll pick you up at eight."

"Wow," Matt said, surprised at the efficiency of the solicitor. "That man knows how to get things done."

Chapter Nineteen

True to his word, O'Doherty picked up Matt at eight o'clock on the dot. Then they drove out to the Twomey farm to collect Claire.

A maid showed them into Kerrigan's study where he was seated behind his desk. He made it a point not to rise to greet his visitors. He was not in the habit of being courteous to adversaries. And he had a personal dislike for the solicitor who'd refused to follow his instructions.

"Take a seat," he said gruffly, "and let's begin."

Unperturbed by Kerrigan's ungraciousness, O'Doherty opened his briefcase. "On behalf of my clients, Mr. Matthew McCartan and Miss Claire Twomey, I have come here prepared to offer you two alternatives regarding the use of the McCartan farm." He slid a folder across Kerrigan's desk. "This is a contract pertaining to the water rights. I think you'll find that the amount is in keeping with standard water rights on the Dingle Peninsula."

Ignoring the boilerplate and legalese, Kerrigan's eyes went immediately to the amount they were seeking. It was as he expected. He'd done his own research and knew to the ha'penny what others were paying for water rights. It was the other sum—the amount for past use of the pond—that took him aback. He looked up at the solicitor and his eye flashed in anger. "This bill for past water rights is ludicrous."

"I think not, Squire. You have been using the McCartan water for thirty years. I have done the research and I know what the cost of water rights has been each year up to the present. I added those sums, plus interest accrued, and that is how I arrived at that sum."

Kerrigan slid the paper back to O'Doherty. "I will agree to the amount for the current use of the water, but as to past use, it's robbery and I won't pay it."

"Well, in that case"—O'Doherty took another folder out and slid it across the desk—"here is a contract to buy the farm."

Kerrigan wouldn't even look at it. "I don't want the damn farm," he said, slamming his fist on the desk. "I just want the water."

O'Doherty shrugged helplessly. "Well, Squire, it has to be one or the other," he said in a tone one uses to explain a simple concept to a child. "Either you pay current and past water rights, or you buy the farm."

"And what if I choose to do neither?" he said.

"Then, as of this moment, you are forbidden to bring your livestock onto to the property of my clients. If you do, I will swear out a warrant for trespass."

"Are you mad? I have to have water for my animals."

"I certainly understand that, Squire. But you're a successful businessman. Surely you know that there is always a cost to doing business. If I must go to court, I'm certain a magistrate would agree with our position."

"This is… is extortion," Kerrigan sputtered.

In spite of himself, O'Doherty had to smile. If ever there was an example of the pot calling the kettle black, it was the squire. "That's a harsh word, Squire, and not at all helpful. I'm trying to negotiate a fair bargain, that's all. If we can't come to a meeting of the minds, then I will be forced to bring the matter before a magistrate."

Kerrigan pointed a boney finger at the solicitor. "Don't think you can scare me with your talk of courts and magistrates. My solicitors can tie up your clients for years. I'll bankrupt them."

O'Doherty took off his glasses and wiped them. "Then you might want to warn your solicitors that they will have to defend you in a criminal matter as well."

Kerrigan's eyes narrowed. "What are you talking about?"

"I'm talking about the attempted murder of my client by a man sent by you."

Kerrigan fell back in his chair. "Attempted murder…? You're mad. He was only to scare him…"

O'Doherty's kindly manner abruptly changed. His face became hard and his voice was low and menacing. "The facts are these, Squire. Your man was armed with a pistol and he pointed it at my client. It was only by the grace of God that my client was able to disarm him before he had a chance to pull the trigger."

Kerrigan's face was purple with rage. "That's a damn lie."

O'Doherty shrugged. "Well, that's why we have courts, isn't it? It'll be up to the magistrate to sort it all out. Mind, it will be a sensational trial. I expect people will come from miles around to see it."

Kerrigan looked stricken, which is what O'Doherty expected. He knew the last thing Kerrigan wanted was to drag this sordid affair into public view.

Kerrigan snapped up the contract and examined it. "Good God, man," he said, slamming the contract on the desk. "The price you're asking is five times more than the damn farm is worth."

"Aye, but the water is good, isn't it?" O'Doherty countered. "And it's the water you need."

Kerrigan was outraged. It was extortion, but what could he do? He was cornered and he knew it. The wily old solicitor had bested him and there was nothing he could do about it. But he wouldn't give him—or McCartan—the satisfaction of seeing him surrender. "I'll need time to think about this."

"As you wish." O'Doherty closed his briefcase and stood up. "We will require an answer within twenty-four hours."

Outside, Matt was still stunned by the performance of his solicitor. He'd had doubts about using the kindly old country solicitor to negotiate with Kerrigan, but what other choice did he have? Still, he'd been prepared to jump in if it looked like O'Doherty was being bullied by Kerrigan. But there had been no need. He shook the solicitor's hand. "Mr. O'Doherty that was masterful."

"Thank you very much."

"Attempted murder? That's a bit of a stretch, isn't it? The gun was inoperable."

O'Doherty's eyes twinkled. "Ah, but Squire Kerrigan didn't know that, did he?"

"Was your asking price really five times what the farm is worth?" Claire asked.

O'Doherty chuckled. "Not at all. It was eight times what the farm is really worth."

"What do you think Kerrigan will decide?" Matt asked.

"I think he'll buy the farm. Paying for water rights year after year would leave him in a vulnerable position. Just as you were afraid he might renege at some time in the future, he would have to worry about you doing the same. The squire is a man who likes everything tight and neat."

~~

That night, over a quiet dinner, Matt described to Karina how O'Doherty had out-negotiated Kerrigan.

Karina grinned. "I told you he was good."

"Yeah, and by the way, thank you for prodding me into checking on the ownership of the farm. I wouldn't have thought of it myself."

"You're quite welcome, kind sir. So what's next?"

Matt made a face. "I've been saving the worst for last. Tomorrow, Twomey and I are going to have a come-to-Jesus meeting."

"I thought you were looking forward to it?"

"I am. But it's not going to be pleasant for Maeve."

"Yeah. I don't know what I would do if I found out after all those years that the man I married had manipulated the whole thing. Then after that, what?"

Matt shrugged. "Go home."

She reached out and squeezed his hand. "I'm gonna miss you, Matt. These last few weeks have been very exciting around here."

"I guess so." He shook his head in amazement. "I can't believe how one innocent letter led to all this."

"They say the pen is mightier than the sword. It's changed your life, Maeve's, Claire's, and all those horrid men who wronged your father. Speaking of horrid men, I met Nora this afternoon at the market. She told me that Father Dunne has asked the bishop for permission to retire. He plans to go to a monastery and spend the rest of his life in prayer and contemplation."

"That foolish old man will have plenty to contemplate."

"He sure will." She placed her hand over his. "Matt, did you find what you were looking for here in Ireland?"

Matt was silent for a moment. "I don't know, Karina. When I came here I didn't know what to expect, but I sure as hell didn't expect what I found. I guess what I learned does explain my father a little better. Now that I know what he went through, I have a better understanding of the way he was. Still, I wish he would have confided in me—or someone. I don't know if I could have helped him, but I know that sometimes just talking it out can help."

"I agree. Catharsis is good for the soul."

"Okay, enough of the doom and gloom. On the brighter side, when are you coming home?"

"I have one more month on my research grant. Then it's back to the states."

"And back to Greenpoint?"

She wrinkled her nose. "Nah. I think I'll get a little apartment downtown somewhere near NYU. What are your plans?"

"I've been hemming and hawing about it since I got out of the service, but I've made up my mind. I'm going to sign up for the GI Bill."

"That's a great idea. What will you study?"

"Law. After watching O'Doherty in action, and seeing the lousy things that Kerrigan was able to get away with, it strikes me as a noble profession. I want to help people."

"And you'll be good at it, too, if you can stand all the lawyer jokes."

Chapter Twenty

The next morning, Matt rode Karina's bike out to the Twomey farm. He didn't see the old man in the fields, so he assumed he was home.

Maeve opened the door and when she saw who it was, came outside and closed the door behind her. "Matt," she whispered, "you shouldn't have come. John is home."

"That's who I came to see."

"About what?"

This was the moment Matt was dreading. She was a wonderful woman and he'd grown very fond of her. He hated to be the one to break her heart. "It's going to be difficult for you Maeve, but there are some things about your husband that you need to know."

She opened the door. "Come in," she said gravely.

Twomey was seated at the table eating. Claire was standing by the stove making tea. He looked up and scowled. "What are you doing here, McCartan?"

"I've come to talk to you."

"I have nothing to say to you," he snarled. "Leave my house."

"I will. Right after you answer a couple of questions for me. Who gave Heaney the money for the butcher shop and why?"

The farmer slowly put his fork down. "I don't know what you're talking about."

"Sure you do. Do you want to tell Maeve why you gave him the money or shall I?"

Twomey jumped up so quickly he banged into the table and spilled his tea. "Outside. We'll talk about this outside."

"No. We'll talk about it right here. I want Maeve and Claire to hear this."

"John, what is he talking about?" Maeve asked.

Twomey waved a hand in dismissal. "'Tis nothing. It was a long time ago. For the love of God, just let it be."

"No, I want to know. You must tell me."

Twomey took a deep breath and glared at Matt. "He needed the money to buy the shop from old man Cahill. I gave him a loan. That's all there was to it."

"No," Matt interjected. "That's not all there was to it. Tell Maeve what you asked him to do for the money."

Twomey glanced around the kitchen like a trapped animal looking for an escape. Finding none, the enraged farmer lunged for Matt.

"John..." Maeve screamed, "what are you doing..."

This was just the excuse Matt had been looking for. Since he'd first learned what he'd done to his father, he'd wanted to give the man a serious beating and now was his chance. He drew back to punch Twomey, but he checked himself when he saw the terror in the old man's eyes. What was the use? A beating couldn't change the past. Nothing could. Matt shoved him back into his chair. "Tell her, Twomey. Tell her what you had Heaney do for the money."

The old man started to sob and covered his face with his calloused hands. "I can't..." he muttered. "I can't..."

Matt almost felt sorry for him. But then he remembered the damage and heartbreak he'd caused everyone. He turned to Maeve. "He gave Heaney the money on the condition he would accuse my father of being an informer."

Ma Maeve's hand shot to her mouth. "Oh, no... John, is this true?"

Still holding his head in his hands, he didn't answer.

Matt continued. "And it was on the strength of Heaney's testimony that they convicted my father and put a price on his head."

Maeve looked dazed. "John," she asked more forcefully, "is this true?"

After a long pause, in a barely audible tone, he mumbled, "Yes..."

"But why would you do such a thing?"

When Twomey didn't answer, Matt answered for him. "Because he wanted to marry you and the only way that could happen was if my father was out of the way."

Maeve fell into a chair and tears welled up in her eyes. "That was a terrible thing you've done, John. And how in heaven's name did you think I would marry you?"

Twomey wiped his runny nose on his sleeve. "I wasn't sure how I would get you to marry me, but when you became pregnant, I knew I could use that to my advantage."

Remembering Father Dunne's confession, she said, "And you promised Father Dunne a new roof if he would convince me to marry you. For the love of God, what were you thinking? You had no right to do such a thing."

"I loved you, Maeve. I always did. I did it for you. I did it for Claire here."

"Bullshit," Matt shouted. "You did it for yourself. You're a selfish old man who ruined a lot of lives for your own self-seeking purposes."

Twomey's chest heaved with the sobs, but he had nothing to say in his defense.

Matt put his hand on Maeve's shoulder. "I'm sorry you had to hear this."

She patted his hand. "I know, Matt," she said softly. "I know…"

He looked at Claire and shrugged. "I guess I'll go now."

Claire, who had observed everything in horrified silence, nodded. "Yes, I think that's best. Goodbye, Matt."

~~

By the time he got back to the hotel, he was physically and emotionally drained. Karina took one look at him and led him into the bar.

"Tough, huh?" she said, pouring him a whisky.

"Tougher on Maeve than on me."

"Is she going to leave him?"

"I don't know. I imagine she's too distraught to think about that right now."

"I have some good news. Mr. O'Doherty called. Kerrigan will buy the farm for the full price."

Matt exhaled in relief. "Well, that's the last loose end. Time to pack up and go home."

"When will you leave?"

"Tomorrow. I don't want to stay in this place another minute. I'll hire a car to take me to Limerick and I'll grab the first plane going to the states."

~~

Early the next morning, Matt walked down to the beach to say goodbye to Hugh before he left. He found the fisherman sitting by his currach mending a net, paying no attention to the light rain that was soaking his cap and jacket.

"Morning, Hugh."

Hugh looked up. "And good morning to you as well. Do you have questions for me this morning?"

"No. I just came to say goodbye. I'm going back to the states."

"Ah, so have you found out everything you wanted to know about your da?"

"Probably not everything, but enough. I want to thank you for all your help."

"'Twas nothing. It was good to think about your da after all these years. Toward the end, it was bad business, but our earlier years were a happy time for us."

132

Hugh stood up and brushed the sand off his trousers. "Well, then."
Matt put his hand out. "Goodbye, Hugh."

The fisherman grasped Matt's hand with his rough weather-beaten hand. "And goodbye to you, Matt McCartan." A small smile played around the old fisherman's mouth. "Are you sure you wouldn't like one last ride on the boat?"

Matt laughed. "No, thanks. My seafaring days are over."

"As you wish." He sat back down on the sand and reached for his net. Matt turned and walked away.

~~

Toward noon, Matt was in his room packing when there was a knock at the door. It was Karina. "You have company."

"Now what?"

"Relax. It's Maeve and Claire. They came to say goodbye."

Matt felt a wave of relief rush over him. When he'd left the farmhouse yesterday, he'd thought that would be the last time he would see either of them. He couldn't blame them if they never wanted to see him again after the devastating news he'd brought them. Even now he wasn't sure he'd done the right thing.

They were waiting in the bar. There was a little redness around Maeve's eyes, but otherwise, she looked well—and she was smiling. A good sign.

Claire gave Matt a hug. "So, brother, you're going back to the states?"

"Yep. Time to go."

Maeve gave him a hug as well. "God bless you, Matt. And thanks for all you've done."

"I don't deserve thanks, Maeve. I'm afraid I've brought you nothing but heartbreak and sadness."

"No, you've brought truth back into my life. And the truth, as painful as it is, is better than all those aching questions that have troubled my mind all these years. Thanks to you, I now know Barry did what he thought was best for us and that he loved me very much."

"Thanks, Maeve. You've made me feel a whole lot better. Claire did you hear we sold the farm?"

"Aye. Karina told me. That's wonderful news."

"I spoke to O'Doherty this morning and instructed him to make the check payable to you."

"But what about your half?"

"I don't need it. I live in a rent-controlled apartment in the city and the government is going to pay me to go to college. Besides, in America the streets are paved with gold. Everybody knows that."

She grinned. "So, I've heard, but that's a fearful huge sum, Matt."

"What'll you do with it?" Karina asked.

"Actually, I've been thinking I would like to go to school in Dublin," she answered tentatively.

"Why not the states," Karina said. "You'll have a brother and a good friend living in New York City. And we have tons of schools to choose from."

"My goodness. I never thought of that. It must be terribly expensive living in New York City, but now, with the farm money…" She trailed off, too embarrassed to continue.

Karina took Maeve's hand. "And what about you, Maeve?" she asked gently. "What are your plans?"

Maeve looked pensive. "I've given it a lot of thought and I've decided I'm going to stay with John."

When she saw the look of outrage on Matt's face, she added, "I know what he did was terribly wrong. But in his own perverse way, I do believe he meant well. And the truth is he did put a roof over our heads and food on the table. As to the past, what's done cannot be undone. All in all, I haven't had a bad life with him."

Matt was about to say she was too good for him, that the old bastard didn't deserve her, but he stopped himself. Who was he to dictate someone else's life?

Just then a car horn sounded. His hired car had arrived. When he came outside, he was dismayed to see his driver was James Casey, the same young man who'd pestered him with questions about America. Now he would have to endure endless questions all the way to Limerick.

Maeve hugged him. "Have a good life, Matthew McCartan," she said.

"And you, too, Maeve. One day maybe you'll visit me in the states."

"Aye. Maybe I will."

He hugged Claire. "Think about what Karina said about coming to the states."

"I will. I will."

He kissed Karina. "Let me know when you're coming home. I'll be waiting for you at the airport."

As the car drove out of the village, Matt turned to look out the rear window. It was hard to believe it was less than three weeks since he'd walked this road into Ballyturan, admiring the beautiful view and imagining that this is what his father saw everyday of his life in Ireland.

"Is San Francisco near New York City?" James Casey asked, pulling Matt out of his reverie.

Matt settled in, resigned to the fact that it was going to be one long ride to Limerick.

"Not even close, James. They're three thousand miles apart."

"Jaysus, Mary, and Saint Joseph," James said in wonderment. "Sure Ireland is barely two hundred miles wide. America must be a great big country."

The End

Author Biography

Michael Grant, a native New Yorker and veteran of the New York City Police Department, has written fourteen novels. He currently lives in Knoxville TN with his wife, Elizabeth, and their golden retriever, Jack. He can be contacted at mggrant08@gmail.com.

BOOKS BY MICHAEL GRANT

In The Time Of Famine
When I Come Home
The Cove
Back To Venice
Line Of Duty
Officer Down
Retribution
Precinct
The Ghost And The Author
Appropriate Sanctions
Stalker
Krystal
Who Moved My Friggin' Provolone?
Dear Son, Hey Ma

45863787R00079

Made in the USA
Charleston, SC
05 September 2015